# Doctor Sinful

DOCTORS OF EASTPORT GENERAL NOVEL

E.M. SHUE

Cover Design by S.L. Sterling of Thunderstruck Cover Design

Formatting by Mountain Rose Press

Editing by Nadine Winningham of The Editing Maven

Cover from AdobeStock Images

Interior Photos from DepositPhoto

www.authoremshue.com

emshue.ak@gmail.com

❀ Created with Vellum

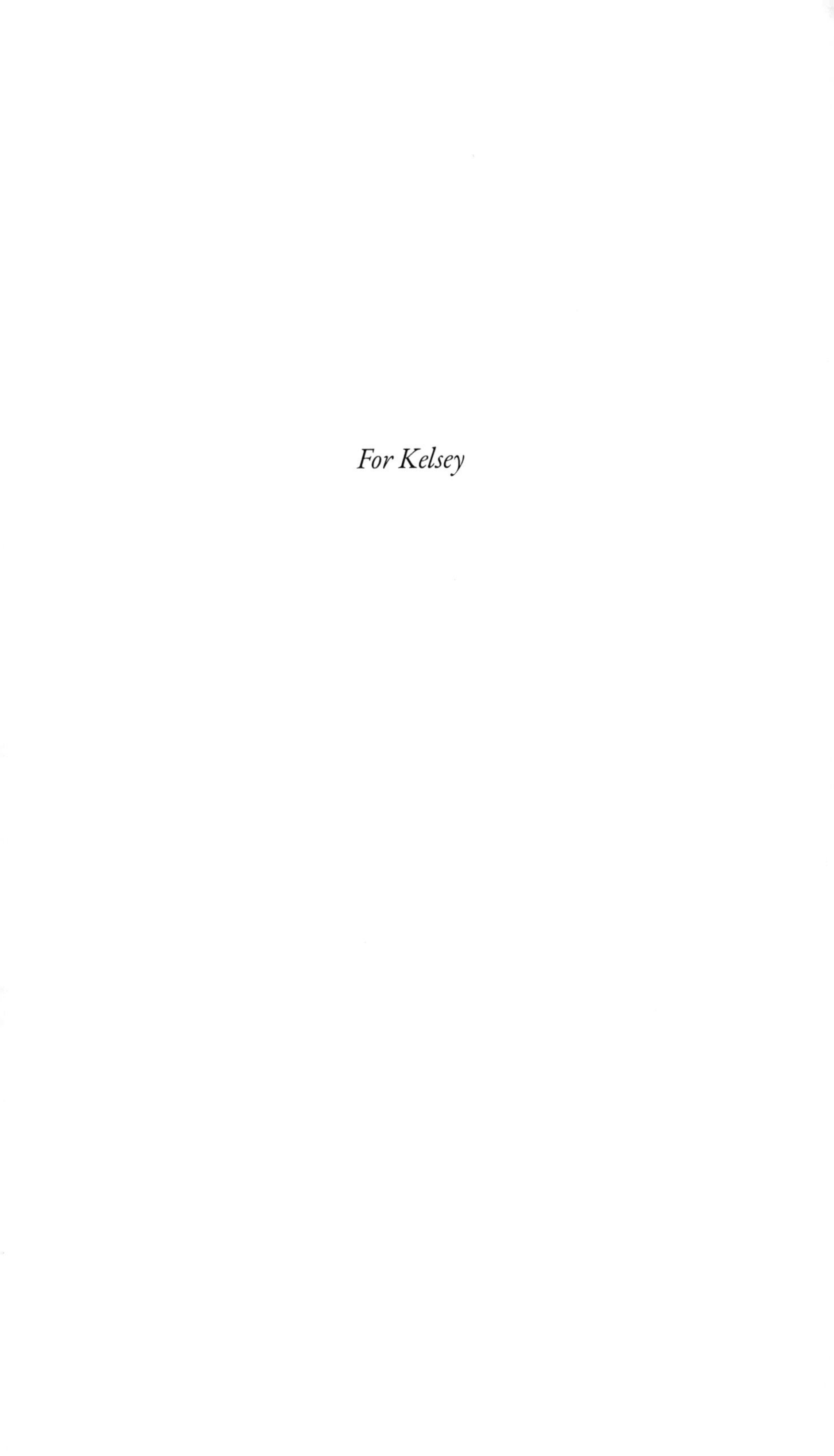

*For Kelsey*

# Blurb

Sinful.

She's been submitting to me for the last few weeks. The perfect little sub. Her body bombshell curvy and eyes that pull me in every time I see them through her mask. When I'm not with her I dream of the things we've done, the things I want to do to her next time.

She only tells me her name is Syn. We never discuss our lives outside this club. I don't know what her real name is. I don't know if she goes home to another person. I've asked her for more. I've asked her to coffee, dinner and just a number to call, but she won't give it to me. I want to know where she goes when she leaves me, does she go home to a full house and a lonely bed like I do?

Being the single father of three active boys and a job as a full-time paramedic keeps me busy. I only have time one night a week that I go to The Satin Room and spend time with my perfect distraction, Syn.

Until the day we bump into each other in the real world, and I realize I want more. She's been under my nose for weeks. I just needed to open my eyes. Now, I'm ready to go for it. But is she ready for me?

The doctor has been paged to the ER where the paramedics have brought you in. Are you ready to check out the halls of Eastport General and the staff. Award-winning author E.M. Shue is back with another sexy doctor and hot paramedic in season two of Doctors of Eastport General.

Join Surprises from E.M. to be kept up to date.

https://bit.ly/SurprisesfromEM

# Chapter One

## EMERSYN

The elevator doors open, and I step out onto the pediatric floor. The momentary quiet is broken by the attendant in the booth as she greets me.

"Hello, Dr. St. James, how are you today?" She smiles at me from behind the glass where most people must stop and check in. I use my badge clipped to the lapel of my lab coat to swipe my way inside.

"I'm doing good today, Rose. How about you?" I smile back at her.

"All's quiet, so I can't complain." We both chuckle, and I hear the giggles of children coming from the family room. I peek through the windows as I pass and see a couple of kids sitting around playing video games with their families and coloring at the table. As I move further onto the floor, I hear more sounds of happiness and soft playing music.

This has been one of the easiest parts about my move

from Boston Community Hospital to Eastport General in Rhode Island. I like that this pediatric unit doesn't solely focus on the children's illnesses and requires the halls to be quiet. Instead, there are fun things and activities for the kids to do, from playing video games to having tutors on staff and even the family room.

I also made this move for my son. He needed a fresh start away from all of his father's issues. My mother was willing to come with us, and we are so much happier here. For now, I'm renting a condo, but we are looking for houses too. I was able to get Sebastian on a hockey team, and he's settling in nicely. I have a better schedule here and get to pick my days off. Yeah, I'm on call, but I'd rather be that than fight several other docs for weekends off. Once the season starts, Bas will have hockey games on Saturdays and I'll be able to see them.

Stopping at the nurses' station, I greet the staff and review my patients' charts. I only have a couple who are admitted. More of my patients come to my office upstairs, where I treat them without them having to stay here. As a pediatric orthopedic surgeon, I help on several different cases, but one of the ones I'm here to check up on today takes the cake.

I've seen the aftermath of child abuse firsthand, but this was one of the worst for me. I'm floored that this little girl and her mother were able to survive this long. I look over the notes and see that little Bailey had a rough night.

I had to perform an emergency hip surgery to repair the damage done after Bailey was hit by a car. A car driven by her own father. He was aiming for the mother, but the little girl took the brunt of the impact. Her mom has several injuries and is being treated here too. Her doctor, the department and hospital heads, and I all agreed to have her placed on this floor with her daughter. This floor is one of the most secure in the hospital, but security has grown even stricter since Bailey and her mom came in yesterday.

I move on to the second chart, a little boy who fell from a tree and broke his arm. I had him admitted because he had an allergic reaction to a medication. He's stabilized and I'll have him discharged later today. I talk to his day nurse and relate my plans before I make my way down the hall toward his room, where I give him and his parents the good news.

Finally, it's time to check in on Bailey. I push my glasses up my nose before stepping through the doorway and past the police officer watching over her.

"Morning," I whisper to Bailey's mom. She gives me a sad smile. Her light brown hair matches her daughter's. "I see it was a little rough last night."

"Yeah, the cast was itching her, and she was in some pain." Bailey trembles in her sleep at the sound of her mother's soft voice.

I move to the bed and check the monitors attached to her, and then I look at the pain medication machine. I'd instructed the night nurse to keep her medicated for the first night to help with the discomfort. I'm going to have to come up with some other things too.

I look down at the sweet little girl. Her face is still a bit dirty, and her long hair is matted. I'll have the nurse bathe her to help with the itching.

"I'm going to have the nurse give her a sponge bath today and wash her hair. Maybe we can braid her hair too." I try to keep my voice down, but Bailey's eyes still flutter open, and she looks up at me. Because of the spica cast to protect her hips and the long length down her broken right leg, she can only be elevated a small amount for right now.

"Hello, Bailey." I smile down at her, and she gives me a fraction of a smile back. I see the pain in her eyes, but I can tell it's not physical. "Are you hurting?" I ask just to confirm.

She shakes her head at me. She's barely spoken since she's arrived, but that doesn't stop me from talking to her.

"How about a bath today, and we can raise your head a bit more?" Her eyes light up some. I think for a moment, trying to remember when Bas was seven and what he was into. "I can also have someone stop by with coloring books and we can get you set up to do that. Sound good?" More light enters her eyes before she looks over to her mom and it dims instantly when she sees the bruises on her mom's face.

"Bailey, baby, it's okay." Her mom moves over and takes her daughter's hand in her free one. Bailey's mom has a broken arm, a few broken ribs, and was beaten really bad.

"Okay, Bailey, I'll stop in and see you later on." I move away and step out to make my notes. It's like a weight to my chest seeing everything that Bailey and her mom went through. The cop on duty sighs loudly.

"It's hard to see that someone could hurt such an innocent little girl." His voice is deep and scratchy. I turn to face him and weakly smile as I nod.

Hours later, after finalizing my chart notes from today's patients, I pull up Bailey's chart. She got a bath, and they were able to wash her hair. Her nurse noted that the social workers were in and out today, along with detectives trying to make their case against her father. I look over her meds. She got them on regular intervals, but I see that she barely ate any food. I'll have to talk to her about how important that will be in her healing.

When I stand from my desk, I arch my back and stretch it. I can't wait until this evening; I've been waiting weeks to go to this new club. My friend Ryan, who helped me get the job here, is a member and couldn't talk enough about it. The club has only been open for a couple of years, but I don't care, as long as it helps me forget about little girls with broken hips from their own father. I slip off my lab coat and put it in the bin to go to cleaning, then I grab my pink leather jacket off the coatrack and slip it on over my sleeveless magenta dress. I grab my pink designer satchel and drop my cell phone into it as I head out of the office.

I say good night to my staff and head down to the

fourth floor to pediatrics. My heels click along the linoleum floor, and I hear raised voices coming from Bailey's room. I move faster and see the police in there.

"This is not the place to do this." I raise my voice just enough to get their attention. Two men turn toward me, and I see Bailey cowering on the bed. I slip between them and her. I look over and see her mother is crying from her bed. At my five-foot-four height, I'm not extremely tall, but my heels give me some height and my presence is commanding. I lower my voice to make it sound more authoritative. "These two have been put through enough. Don't you think?" I tip my head slightly and feel Bailey's small hand grip my jacket at my back. It's the first time she's initiated any contact between us.

"Ma'am, we can't find the assailant and can't keep security on the room indefinitely." One of the detectives takes me in. I watch his eyes move from my feet up to my face. I know his look. My voice has a heavy huskiness to it; I'd have no problems getting hired as a phone-sex operator. My body is curvy and trim. I have larger breasts that his eyes rove back down to. The urge to tell him my eyes are north of my boobs is great, but instead I tip my chin.

"I believe hospital administration will have something else to say about that. We were assured our patients would be safe. Isn't that your job? And it's *Doctor* to you. Doctor St. James." I step back, not wanting him close to me.

"Sorry, Dr. St. James," the other detective says. "You're correct. We'll make sure an officer is left here until we apprehend the victim's father." He puts a hand to his partner's shoulder and pulls him back. I look up at the first detective again. He's still checking me out. He's not ugly, but he's not handsome either. However, something about him doesn't sit right with me. I wait until they leave the room before I turn to Bailey.

"Are you okay?" I ask her softly. She grabs a hold of my jacket. I notice that I was wrong earlier. Now that her hair is cleaned, it's such a pale brown it's almost blond, whereas her mother's is still brown.

"He's going to kill us," she says so softly I barely hear her.

"Not if I can help it," I promise her.

Carefully, I check her over, and she keeps touching my bag that I'd set on her bed when I squared off with the detectives. I smile when I see her trace the letters on the side of it.

"My mom got it for me as a gift when I graduated from medical school," I tell her. "Do you like purses and bags?"

She nods and smiles at me. I know it's not a good idea as the thought goes through my head, but I'm bringing her one of my older bags tomorrow. She has nothing and I can't stand it.

Before I leave the floor, I make sure the nurse knows to give me a call if there are any problems. I head down to the employee parking lot, where my new car is waiting for me, and then I head home to spend time with my family before heading to the club for some real fun.

# Chapter Two

TREVOR

It's been a long several days. The boys have started hockey practice, and work has been busy. It's like the August rain is bringing out the crazies. I need a release. I park my truck in the parking lot across from the Satin Room. My sister, Lorelei, has the boys, and this is the only night I have to myself. The doorman, Boz, opens the heavy blacked-out doors. He's a huge guy, a good solid four inches taller than my six-foot-two and wider than me. He used to play hockey professionally before he got cut for unnecessary roughness.

"Hey, Trevor." His voice sounds awful. It's so gruff, I always imagine him being in the *Godfather*.

"What up, Boz?"

"The sky, my fly, and my cock. You should see the new little sub that just started." He chuckles. "I'd tap her if she were a bit bigger. Nice little petite one with amazing eyes," he shares, and I nod.

"I'll take a look." He doesn't like petite girls, says he'll break them as big as he is. I'm all about the eyes, so his comment about hers gets to me. They say eyes are windows to the soul, but for me it's more than that. I've been fucked over a couple of times. I have an ex that did a number on me, as they say. Jas, one of my paramedic friends from the station, called her a raging bitch when she heard the stories from my sister. I don't share that much about my past. Not only is it to make sure I don't talk bad about her in front of the boys, but because I don't talk ill of the dead either.

I check in at the registration desk and then move into the main chamber. When Leif and Erika started this business, people said they wouldn't make anything of it. Little did those idiots know that Eastport has its share of freaks that don't like to travel all the way to Providence or out of state for some fun. I've known for years I was a Dom. After my ex left, I started going to a few underground places. Leif had told me his idea about the Satin Room one day when he was working on one of my tattoos. I thought it was brilliant.

Now here we are, and I'm one of the members of the board. I do remember seeing an application for a new sub from Boston. I didn't meet her though because of my schedule.

As I work my way through the club, I observe the cross is in use and a whip-master is showing off their techniques. I head toward the bar and order a beer. I look down the polished wood to a stool where a bombshell beauty is seated. I know instantly that this is the woman Boz was talking about. She's in a black mesh paneled see-through long-sleeve bustier style top. It ends in a skirt that brushes the top of her thighs. I can barely make out the sexy little shorts that cover her ass. I want her to stand so I can see if her fuller cheeks will hang out the bottom of them. My mouth starts to water with the thought of biting into her sweet cheeks before I bury my tongue deep inside her core. Her long dark brown hair is in waves around her shoulders and hanging down her back. I can picture my hands fisted in her strands. My cock is rock-hard. I move toward her as my gaze follows her shapely muscled legs down to her five-inch platform heels.

I drag my eyes back up her body to her sexy full breasts. They must be at least a D-cup.

"You're new." My voice comes across deep and husky sounding. People think I smoke from the sound of it, but I don't. I work out and I'm extremely healthy. I also used to play hockey back in the day but not professionally. I watch her beautiful hazel green eyes as they drag over my body.

"I am." There's a slight tremor in her voice, and it adds an extra sexiness to her. She's got a voice that makes me want to drop and beg her to talk to me.

I hold out my hand to her. "Trevor." She's in a mask that is obscuring some of her face and I wish I could see it all. But the black next to her eyes makes them look even greener.

"Syn." She holds out her hand, and when our palms slide together something deep inside me comes awake. A feeling I haven't felt in too long. She trembles and a flush works its way across the top of her breasts.

"Join me." I wave to the table I set my beer on before I approached her. The low tabletops are wood and as shiny as the polished bar. It was Erika's idea to have the wood offset all the black and red of the room.

"Okay," she answers me as if it was a request. It wasn't. I wanted to see how much of a sub she was. She wants to take direction. I reach for her wine glass with one hand and slide the other against the small of her back. Her hips flare wide, but her waist is tiny enough that my large mitt takes up most of her lower back. My pinky finger rests right above the crack of her ass. When I direct her to the seat, I step back and take her in from behind before I move the second chair to sit right next to her. I'm not letting any other Dom make a move on her.

She is mine.

She leans back and crosses one leg over the other, and I reach across to rest my hand on her knee. She doesn't cringe back from my dominate move.

"Are you nervous?" I watch her closely to see if she'll try to hide the truth, but she openly stares back at me before she drops her gaze for a moment. When she looks back up, she bites that luscious bottom lip as she looks me in the eye again.

"It's been weeks since I submitted to anyone. I'm not afraid of you." I feel the urge to ask her who she submitted to before. She must sense my anger at the thought of another Dom controlling her. "That was at the club I attended back in Boston." It's the first personal thing she's given me because I'm not sure her name is real.

"Would you like to play?" I slide my hand down to her thigh while watching every reaction of her body. Her breathing increases, her pulse flutters under her skin, and the flush from earlier has worked its way up her neck.

I want to follow that pink tinge under her beautiful slightly tan skin. I see a tattoo peeking out from under her skirt on her hip and I want to lick that too.

"Yes," she says, and I reach for the new tablets that we approved to make it easier to learn hard and soft limits. I enter my passcode and then her name. Up pops all her information. What she likes. What she doesn't. Even her contract history. That surprises me.

"You're not under contract with anyone else? You've been a sub for five years though? And never been under a contract for longer than a month or so." I'm shocked because she's extremely beautiful. Any Dom would snatch her up, not just because of her looks but the fact she submits beautifully so far.

"I just moved here from out of state. I also have a very demanding job and life outside of the club. I can't give more than one night a week. I only need the release every so often." Another kernel of information.

We sit for a bit longer talking about her limits and mine. When I hand her the tablet, she presses her thumb to the area stating she'll be with me tonight. It's for ours and the business's protection. If either of us enter into more of a contract, it will be on file here too. I take the tablet from her and set it back on the table. I want a long-term contract with her, and I too haven't been under one in a while. I take subs for a couple of months at a time as I don't usually want a woman for that long. The last woman I had in my life who wasn't my sister or mother didn't want to be in my life, so I try not to get into more with anyone else now.

I'm ready to play with her and see how much I can make her body flush while she comes. I take a final swig of my beer before I stand and hold out my hand to her.

Emersyn

I sit there for a moment before I take another sip of my wine. When Trevor walked up to me, I thought I was in a dream. I turned around and looked up his large, toned, and muscular body. He took my breath away. He's over six feet tall and wide. He's dressed in all black. Black jeans and a black button-down that is open at the collar, exposing a light sprinkling of dark chest hair. I want to drag my hands through it. I'm not normally a beard girl, but his mid-length scruff is sexy and I want the burn across my body. It's dark, like his hair that is shaved on the sides and brushed straight up in a spiky but soft style. A yearning starts in my stomach and settles in my core. This man is projecting power and desire. I want it all.

After we sat at the table, I thought he wanted to just

talk, but I felt his eyes brush my body as if he was caressing me. The sensation caused my skin to erupt in gooseflesh. When he looked at my information and questioned me about contracts, I thought he was going to get up then, but he didn't. I did notice from his profile he doesn't stay under contract for very long either. I also saw that he's on the board and listed as a training Dom for the club.

I must be taking too long because he moves his hand and slides it under my hair, where he wraps it around the back of my neck. The show of dominance causes my already damp panties to practically combust. I stand and let him lead me from the bar area. He guides me up the stairs and down the catwalk, stopping at the last door. I'm aware each board member has their own private suite. He releases me to pull a skeleton key from his pocket and slide it into the lock, then he pulls the large sliding barn door open.

The room is decked out in all black. Black satin sheets, black candles, black sofa, and even a black area rug on the floor. His hand returns to my neck and he directs me into the room.

Once inside, he releases me again and moves past me. I watch as he removes things from a cabinet. I'm curious but know if I ask he won't tell me. I'll also get a spanking, something I badly need, which makes me contemplate whether or not to ask. His voice breaks me from my thoughts before I can decide.

"Kneel."

I drop into the submissive pose with my knees

together, back straight, and eyes down. My hands rest on my thighs as I wait for his next command. He moves around the room, and I want to look up when I hear the thump of things falling. But as a good submissive, I don't. My eyes are focused on the floor when his now bare feet move into my line of sight. I didn't know men's feet could be sexy, but his are. He's still in his black jeans, and I keep my focus on his strong feet.

"I want to pull your hair, but I don't want it to interfere with what I have planned for you. Can you braid it?" He hands me a ponytail elastic and I take it without looking up.

I finger brush my hair and divide it into three sections before I weave it into a thick braid down my back. I secure it with the elastic and push it back when I'm done.

"Good girl. Now stand." He holds out a hand for me.

As I stand up, my eyes track from his bare feet up his long legs to the waist of his black jeans, which are now unbuttoned. My gaze lands on the happy trail of hair that disappears into his opened jeans. I want to touch. I want to lick, but I keep my focus on his commands.

When I'm fully standing in front of him, he slides his palm along the side of my face and tips my head back.

"One of your hard limits is kissing, but I want to sip from your beautiful lips." He looks me in the eye, and I want to say yes. I set that as a limit because kissing is so intimate, and I wouldn't be able to keep a distance if I allowed it.

"I just can't."

"Why?" His brow raises.

"Please, Sir, I want to do this with you, but I can't give you that." I can't tell him that if I kiss him, I'm afraid I'll lose myself. I already feel a pull to him I've never felt before with another Dom. I can't tell him my ex-husband fucked me over in ways that I'm still paying for. Literally. I can't tell him that kissing is more intimate than the act of fucking. "Yellow." If I say "red," I know he'll stop.

He leans forward and holds me firm as I start to pull away. His lips brush my forehead and I sigh from the contact. It's been so long since a man has kissed me, but that kiss right there rocks me to the core. It's tender, and his lips are soft but firm.

"Come." He pulls away and takes my hand. He leads me over to the wall with a stripper pole next to it and where restraints hang from the ceiling. He steps back and crosses his arms, his legs braced shoulder-width apart. He's intimidating in this stance, and if I didn't already feel comfortable and safe with him, I'd worry. "Show me." His voice has a gruffness to it that I'm assuming is from restraining himself. He waves his hand up and down my body.

I swallow, my confidence leaving me. I know I'm sexy, but I also have a softness that he doesn't. I do Pilates and yoga. I don't run. I don't work out all the time because I don't have time for it. He's all solid muscle, looks like he barely has any body fat.

The song in the background changes to "Porn Star Dancing" and I get an idea. I've never done this before in order to seduce someone. I move to the pole and start dancing as the song plays. I'm swaying my hips and moving around as I slowly lower the zipper of my bustier. I lick my lips, just like the song says, and go for it. I drop my top to the floor, followed by my skirt. I'm left in nothing but my short, tight black panties and boots. I grab the pole and pull myself up, hanging there for a moment before I flip off. I took a pole dancing workout class back in Boston almost a year ago. Apparently, I didn't forget anything I learned from that class. I lean against the pole and peek at him as the song comes to an end.

Trevor moves toward me and pins me to the pole. "I want to take those sexy as fuck red lips, but instead I'm going to spank you for pushing my limit." He spins me around. "Grab the pole and bend over." I do as he says as he moves away for only a moment. Then the first smack falls across the full part of my butt. He moves to the next cheek and strikes it with the crop. "How many is that, Syn?"

"Two, Sir."

"Count."

The crop connects with my skin a couple more times. By the time we reach five, I'm in a haze of desire. When the next smack doesn't come, I almost beg for it, needing the release.

"To the wall. Now," he orders, and I move in front of the restraints.

I stand there, taking him in. His chest is heaving, and his jaw is tight. I've truly pushed him. I don't know what he's going to do to me next. I gave him permission, and he knows everything I like and don't. I want to kiss him and take that anger from him, but I stick to my guns.

Trevor raises my wrists over my head and secures them together to the ceiling restraints. He pushes me back against the wall and pulls a blindfold from his back pocket with a smirk on his lips. He slips it over my head and the mask covering my face. I can't see, and the depravation of my sight turns me on more. I like to have my vision blocked, so this causes me to almost combust with need. I can't wait to feel what he does next.

The hum of a vibrator reaches my ears over the thumping rock music now playing. His choice in music is eclectic and varying. As soon as the vibrator is pressed against my sternum, all thoughts but it leave my mind. He moves it down my cleavage between my breasts and the vibration against my bone causes me to dampen my panties more. I'm ramped up now.

He moves it to my breast and circles a nipple as warm moisture surrounds the other. I moan and arch my body toward him. He bites my nipple and I'm climbing into the sky ready to explode.

"Don't come until I tell you," he orders as he switches sides. "These sexy full breasts are more than a mouthful, so I'm going to have to really love them up." I squeeze my thighs together in order to ease my throbbing clit. "Nuh-uh, Syn." His voice is so deep my clit throbs more.

The vibrator now slides down my stomach and circles my belly button before it reaches my panty covered core. I feel him shift to his knees. I can't see him, but I look down my body sure that he's there. I throw my head back and cry out when he presses the vibrator against my clit through my panties, but I don't come yet. I need this release, and I'm so close. He pulls it away, and I start to descend that mountain I was climbing. I can't take it. I'm about to beg until I feel his hands wrap around my hips at the top of my panties. He slowly drags them down my legs, his fingers caressing as he goes. He pulls them over my boots and off. My breathing increases as I wait for what is coming next.

The vibrator starts up again, and then it's pressed against my throbbing clit. I almost come with that one touch. It's too much. I thrash my head side to side and can't stop the words that fall from my mouth.

"Please, Sir. I want to come." Every second of time I've been with Trevor has been foreplay to this moment.

"Your voice and those words are so sexy. Say it again."

My voice goes huskier, and I beg him again. I'll beg him in every language I know if it gets me the release I need.

"Not yet, my Syn," he says, and then the vibrator is entering me, ramping me higher. His lips latch onto my clit and he sucks me deep. I cry out. The orgasm is right there clawing at me, wanting to burst, and I'm afraid I can't stop it. Everything is gone and my body tightens up. I've had other Doms withhold orgasms but nothing like this. I'm so close, I could burst in a small breeze. My head is thrashing and I'm begging. I don't know what words I'm spewing, but I can't stop them.

Trevor grips my hips and hoists me up. "Come, Syn," he orders as he slams into me and groans. I couldn't stop my orgasm if I wanted to. His cock looked impressive behind his jeans, but feeling the long and thick length inside of me is pure bliss. He slams into me over and over as I cry out until nothing is left. No words or sounds escape my throat. He continues to move in and out as my head lolls against the wall.

# Chapter Three

TREVOR

Her body is flushed. Her head moves to the side and my lips are on her throat. Her taste is on my tongue as I move in and out of her. I had to have a taste, I couldn't stop myself when I smelled her and saw her desire dripping from her. It's usually a hard limit for me because, like with her and kissing, it's too intimate. But I couldn't stop myself. She's deep in subspace and cries out again when I come in the condom. My hips stop moving and I hold myself in her tight pussy. I need to pull out and take care of her. She whimpers as I slowly withdraw from her body. I reach up to release her arms. They fall onto my shoulders and wrap around me. I carry her over to the sofa, where I wrap her in a blanket and sit with her on my lap. I need to focus on her and will take of the condom shortly. Her head lolls back on my shoulder, and I pull the blindfold off. Her eyes are closed behind her mask. The temptation to lift and look at her face fully is almost too much, but I respect her privacy and gently rub her arms and shoulders under the blanket. She's so soft, and her slightly tan olive skin is practically glowing from the flush still on it. My beard burn along her neck is a moment of pride I can't hide. I want to thump my chest and parade her around the floor.

She stirs as she comes out of subspace. I watch her lined eyes open. Her makeup is still in place.

"Would you like me to get you some water?"

"Please." Her voice is soft and full of sleep.

I gently sit her next to me before I move to take care off the condom and grab her a water bottle from the small fridge hidden in one of the cabinets. I fix my jeans, leaving the top button undone, and make my way back to her. Her head is resting against the back of the sofa. I know I pushed her a bit, but I couldn't stop myself when she pushed me with that striptease. Her body is sexy. I was lost the minute she started dancing.

I lift her up again and sit with her on my lap. I like her in my arms. I shouldn't, but I do. She shudders when she takes a deep breath and then reaches for the water I opened. Her lips wrap around the top and I can imagine them wrapped around my cock. I can't believe I'm ready for her again when my cock stirs to life. But she's not ready, so I continue to take care of her as she slowly starts to come back. Her body is so relaxed into mine and it feels good. For once I like a woman in this position. I've done this for past subs, but I'm not known as a gentle kind of guy. After everything Portia, my ex, put me through, I don't like women to cling to me. But Syn isn't her, and I realize how much I've missed just having a woman cuddling with me.

She takes another deep breath and looks at me. Her eyes are brighter, and the flush has left her skin.

"I guess that's the end," she says softly as she starts to move off my lap. I grip her hips to hold her still.

"It doesn't have to be." I can't believe I'm going to ask her this. "Meet me again?"

"I can't until next week. I only have one night a week I can be here."

"Me too. Can I get your number and we can arrange to meet?"

"No." She smiles shyly and looks down at her hands in her lap. "May I get dressed, Sir?" she asks me. I watch her as she pulls that full bottom lip into her mouth and bites it. It slides from between her pretty white teeth, and I want to bite it too. I start to lean toward her. "Red." Her words stop me, and she pulls back from me. "I can't," she says, and I'm so shocked when she rises from my lap and moves across the room to her top. I sit there in stone silence as she puts it on. I realize I must have fallen into a trance when I notice she's fully dressed and entering the adjoining bathroom.

"I'm sorry." I rise from the sofa and move toward her. "It was a reflex. I'll be here at the same time next Tuesday. Meet me for a drink and we can decide if we'll scene again." I want to reach for her and pull her back against me. She's so much smaller than me, but she's perfect.

"Okay." Her voice is soft and has a bit of trepidation to it.

"I won't push that limit with you, but I want to continue to scene with you in the future." I slide my hands along her face and into her hair. She grips my chest and I tip her head back. I know she's going to think I'm going for her lips again, but as I lower my head, I tip hers toward me and I kiss her forehead. I linger for a moment, trying to convey my apology. "I really don't want to hear you say red again if I can help it. Okay? Now let me walk you to your car." I pull away and move back to where I dropped my shirt. When I turn back around, she's still standing there staring at me. She is working those sexy lips, biting them, and I so want to take them between my teeth.

"Okay," she says, her voice again soft.

I quickly slip my socks and boots on. I take her hand and lead her from the room. I lock up, knowing that the staff will come in and clean tomorrow like they always do during the day. I direct her to the stairs closest to us and the main door, so she isn't walking along the main floor with the just fucked look and no collar. My hand goes to her lower back when we get to the top of the stairs, and I direct her down. She hasn't spoken since we left the suite. I know she's a little freaked out by having to use her safe word and me trying to kiss her. When we reach the lobby, I wait while she gets her jacket—a long wool trench that covers her outfit. Her hair is still braided. Boz smirks when we pass him, and I slightly shake my head, not wanting him to comment.

"I'm over there." Syn's voice is barely over a whisper, and I know it's because she's worried about me finding out more information about her. She's not scared of me. She's worried though.

"Let's go. I'm over here too."

We move toward a white GMC SUV. It's not one of the large ones but more of a crossover style. It's new by the paper plate in the back window. She clicks the key fob and the lights blink as the driver's side door unlocks and the interior lights turn on. I like that she has that security feature on. She turns to me at the rear of the car and rests against it.

"I didn't mean to say red. I'm just not ready for that. I don't want to give you all my baggage, but I was hurt in the past."

"Syn, I'll take whatever I can get of you right now." I lean into her, pressing her against the car. My body is tight against hers and I'm ready to take her again. "I wish you'd send me a text to let me know you make it home okay."

"I'm not ready for that. This world"—she waves her hand toward the club—"has never been a part of my real world." I get what she's saying.

I lean down and kiss her cheek softly before I kiss the tip of her nose.

"Good night, my beautiful Syn," I tell her softly.

"Good night, Trevor. I really enjoyed tonight and meeting you."

I step away from her and direct her to the driver's door. I watch as she opens it and gets in. When she buckles up, I step back and watch as she starts the car. She looks back at me through the window and smiles. Her whole face lights up. She pulls away and I can see her arm moving as she removes her mask. I move to my truck and head home.

I pull up to the large house I bought with money I got from my parents after Portia died. The house has five bedrooms and an attached in-law apartment with a single bedroom. It also has a three-car garage for the main house and another two-car garage attached to the apartment. It's extravagant, but I like that each of my boys has their own room. I even have a guest room in the basement. My sister stays in the apartment, so she is close to help with the boys when I need her to.

I look at all the gym equipment and off-road vehicles in the other stalls of the garage as I park. Moving through, I make my way inside to the master suite that is close to the garage. I take a shower, hating that I have to wash Syn from my body.

I look at my large king-size bed my sister and mother decorated in creams and browns. There's a cream-colored sofa by the big window overlooking the backyard and the coast in the distance. I sit on the side of the bed and think of everything I need to do tomorrow. Lorelei will get the boys up and off to school for me since I work the graveyard shift tomorrow. I've worked for Eastport Ambulance

Service since shortly after my oldest son, Brooklyn, was born.

Portia and I got pregnant while I was in college. It wasn't planned but we had made the best of it. I switched majors and became an EMT, then moved to paramedic. She continued to go to school for a few months after he was born, then dropped out. I proposed, but she didn't want to get married just because we were having a kid. We lived in a small apartment at the time, and I did the best I could. After the twins, Hayden and Holdyn, came three years later, Portia started pushing away. She left a month after their first birthday and died of a drug overdose three years later. Without my family I would have given up some days.

Leaning back in the bed, I stare at the ceiling and think of Syn. Her body and eyes fill my mind. I reflect on her perfect submission to me up until I tried to kiss her. She's everything I've looked for in a woman, but I can't trust these feelings yet. They are too fast and too soon. I can't let another woman blindside me like Portia did.

My hand slides across the bed to the empty side. The coolness of the sheets settles like a lump in my stomach. I wish I had Syn's body next to mine, settling into me. I want her to be my little spoon. My last thought before I fall asleep is of Syn's body pressed against mine. Tomorrow all three of my boys have hockey practice and I'll be too busy to focus on anything but work and my family. That is the hope, at least.

Emersyn

I watch him in the rearview mirror as he moves to a large truck. It's exactly the type of vehicle I'd expect him to drive. I think about everything that happened. He took me so deep into subspace all the tension has left my body. I almost let him kiss me.

I loved the way he touched me when he led me out of the club. His hand moved from the back of my neck to my lower back. He used his body to shield people from seeing me. Even the doorman didn't say anything to us. I liked that he was a gentleman and walked me to my car. It was more of a date than just sex with him.

On the drive to the condo I share with my son and mother, I think of everything. After my divorce, I explored BDSM because I'd always had cravings my ex-husband would call me a freak for liking, but now I know I'm perfectly normal. I've never had a long-term Dom. I'm honestly not sure if I'm looking for one. Getting rid of my ex was hard enough, and I'm still not entirely free of him. I have one more week to go, then I won't have to pay him alimony anymore. As of the fourth of September, I'll have an extra fifteen hundred dollars in my bank account. Not to mention the five hundred I was paying him in child support for the two nights a month he had Bas. Caleb no-showed at our last court appearance, and the judge ruled since Caleb wasn't exercising his visitation—and hadn't for more than three months—I didn't have to pay him child support anymore. For five years that deadbeat has been living off of me. Between all the financial support ending and my new wages at the hospital, I was able to buy this new GMC I'd been eyeing and researching for years. I can also start looking at houses to buy. My mother tried to give me money to help pay for it, but I wouldn't let her. She's helped me so much already by moving in and helping with Sebastian. I wouldn't have been able to get my medical license and work without her. She raised me and has been there for Bas too.

I pull up to the high-rise condo and drive down to the underground parking. After locking the car, I move to the elevator and take it up to my floor. Quietly, I move through the three-bedroom condo to my master suite, where I go straight to the bathroom. I look at myself in the mirror. My large D-cup breasts are barely contained in the material of my top. My hips flare into the perfect hourglass figure. After my divorce, I learned to love my body. I no longer heard my ex's constant criticism about my boobs being too big or my hips and ass still looking like I was carrying our son. It took a lot to not hear his voice, but in the last five years I've been happier.

My hair is still in the messy braid that Trevor asked me to put it in to keep it back. I'll remember that if I scene with him again. I strip out of the revealing outfit and move to the shower, where I use my heavy-duty makeup remover to remove the eyeliner and lip stain. They didn't smudge, which is why I spend the money I do on them.

As the water slides down my body, I think of everything that happened tonight. As soon as those heavy wooden doors opened, I thought I was stepping into what Alice would think is Wonderland.

I climb into bed and fall fast asleep until Bas crawls into bed with me after a nightmare. I need to get him into counseling to discuss what happened with his father in the end. He's been better since we moved here.

# Chapter Four

EMERSYN

"Hello, Dr. St. James," Bailey says happily from the bed. She's raised up higher and is getting better. She's been here for four days now, and I'm discharging her today. "Did you hear my momma and I are moving into a new apartment?" Her smile is so big it lights up the room.

"I did." I smile back as my excitement matches hers. "Do you have your own bedroom?"

"Yes. I'm going to decorate in pink."

"That's my favorite color. Want to see a picture of my room?" I pull my cell from my pocket and click on my photos. "See." I show her the picture I took of my room when I finished decorating it. I love decorating, it's something that calms me. My bed has a white-and-rose gold comforter with pale pink accent pillows. At the foot of the bed are two white chairs with pink-and-gold pillows that say "love" in script on them.

"I love that. Look, Momma." She gets her mother's attention. Social services has been working with them and is placing them in a secure location. I'm glad they will be protected.

I turn to the computer on the wall and finish entering her discharge instructions as they discuss their new apartment. I'm glad the social worker got them a handicap accessible place as Bailey will be in a wheelchair for a couple more weeks, at least.

My cell pings, and I look to see a text from my mom.

MOM

Need you to call me ASAP

"Okay, ladies. You take care of yourselves. I'll see you in my office in two weeks for a checkup." I say goodbye and step out into the hall, where I dial my mother's cell.

"What's up?"

"Sebastian got in a fight at school. I'm at my appointment and can't leave. Can you pick him up?"

"Oh my goodness. What happened?" I move to the elevator to head up to my office to grab my things.

My mother hangs up after explaining that Bas and two of his friends got in a fight with another kid. I'm so angry my body is vibrating with emotion. I really could use another release with Trevor. It's only been two days and I can't stop thinking of him. Maybe I will take him up on the offer to scene again on Tuesday.

I'm stressed out waiting for the other shoe to drop. I had petitioned to the court that visitation needed to be altered with my ex-husband. The last time Bas came home after visiting his dad, he had bruises he wouldn't talk about. My attorney has fought to get a protective order in place. Finally, earlier today the judge agreed. I'm thankful we were able to switch to a different judge who isn't friends with my ex's parents. Caleb is going to be pissed as soon as he finds out, not that he was ever an active father. When Bas was born, Caleb told me he didn't know how to care for him. He would change a diaper once in a while and would hold him a bit, but my mother and I were his primary caretakers. We lived with her because she didn't want me to drop out of medical school. I didn't want to get pregnant when I did, but it happened. Now everything I do, even working, is for Bas to have a better life. He deserves everything.

I pull up to Eastport Elementary School and park in the visitor parking area. The late August weather is windy but still warm. I dressed in something fall inspired today. My green skirt goes to my knees and has a slight split up the back. My cream-colored shell style top is sheer at the shoulders. Under my lab coat no one would know that, but I can feel a slight chill when I walk across the parking lot. Wanting to get to my son as fast as I could, I left my jacket at the office.

Bas has been acting up, but for him to use his fists isn't appropriate. I'm not only upset with him, I'm concerned as to why. My green heels click against the linoleum floors of the hall. I turn into the office and find Bas seated with two boys who are obviously identical twins. Their hairstyles are slightly different, and one has a slightly fuller face.

"Sebastian Christos St. James, what were you thinking!" I raise my voice and three sets of eyes focus on me. Bas has a busted lip and a mark on his cheek. One of the other two boys is not only sporting a black eye but what could be a broken nose. His brother only has a busted lip. All three are covered in grime from rolling in the dirt.

"Mom, he started it. He jumped Hays. Dyne and I just had to defend him." Bas waves his arm toward the office door, which opens as the principal steps out with another boy. The boy is bigger than the three boys seated.

"Dr. St. James, I'm sorry you had to come down here. I've got it all taken care of. These three"—she points at Bas and his friends—"will be out of school for the rest of the week." Her grip tightens on the shoulder of the boy next to her. "This one, however, will be out for another week and then a week of in-school suspension when he returns. He jumped Hayden, and I don't put up with that. I've heard from these three that he has been bullying them all too."

That explains Sebastian's attitude lately.

"Okay, as long as it's taken care of. Come on, Bas, let's go." I direct him to follow me, but he stops to talk to the two boys he was sitting with.

"Hopefully you don't get into too much trouble. My mom is a doctor if you want her to look you over, Hays." I can't hold back the smile that he's offering me to help his friend.

"No, it's okay, our dad is a paramedic."

I nod at the boys and wave my hand to Bas. "Come on, honey. You'll have to go to the hospital with me. I still have some charts to finish up. Boys, if you need me or your parents want to talk, just call this number." I hand one of them my card that has my cell on it.

"Bye, Dr. St. James," the boys say at the same time. "Bas, call tomorrow," the one named Hays says. He has the shorter hair and fuller cheeks.

"I'll try." Bas follows me out to the car, and we head back to the hospital.

Trevor

I pull up to the school as a white car that looks a lot like Syn's pulls away. It doesn't have the paper plate but an actual one and I shake my head. I can't get her out of my head and it's driving me crazy. Now I have to deal with my boys, and I'm pissed. Fighting is not tolerated. They will be running laps around the yard when we get home.

They look up when I stomp into the office, and I cringe when I see Hayden's face.

"Hays, what the hell happened?" I demand. A boy seated across from them chuckles. He stops laughing when I turn on him and glare.

"Mr. Myer, this boy jumped Hayden." The principal points to the boy who was just laughing. "Holdyn and their friend, Sebastian, jumped in to protect him. As I already explained to Dr. St. James, Sebastian's mom, I'm only suspending your sons and Sebastian for tomorrow. They can return on Tuesday after the holiday. As for Billy, he will be suspended longer for starting the fight and bullying."

"Bullying?" I turn to the boy and give him the evil eye again. "You need to burn off some energy, I'm sure the janitor can find something for you to do."

"Excuse me, that's my son," a voice I recognize says. I turn to see Hilary, one of the moms on the opposing hockey team. She's been asking me out for years now. I turn her down because I know what she wants and she ain't going to get it. Definitely not now that I have Syn.

"Come on, boys." I wave my fingers at them. "I have to get you cleaned up and fed before I have to work tonight." They jump up and move toward me. As I step around Hilary, she touches my arm and I pull back from her.

"Come on, Trevor, let's take all the boys out. Show them bygones be bygones."

"No thank you. Lorelei has dinner cooking already." She knows Lorelei is my sister and is usually at all the practices. I make the games though.

I load the boys up into my truck and head off toward home.

"Hays, are you okay?" I ask as I look at him in the rearview mirror.

"I'm okay, Dad. If you could just fix my nose." I nod in response.

"What really happened?" Hayden is my soft soul, as I call him. He cares about everyone and everything. He's more sensitive than his brothers.

"Billy was calling Bas names and I told him to stop. When the gym teacher turned his back, he literally jumped on top of me." Billy is bigger than my boys, who are also big for their age.

"Who is Bas?"

"He's the new boy who just moved here. His mom was able to get him on our team, so we'll be playing hockey together. He played back in Boston, where he lived before moving here. He's neat. His grandma comes to pick him up, but we saw his mom today."

"She's really pretty, Dad," Holdyn supplies, and I just shake my head. He's been listening to Lorelei too much and thinks I need to start dating. "I'm serious, Dad, she's hot, as they call it."

"Dyne, I'm not interested," I grumble. After the last couple of days, I'm only interested in one woman, and she's a perfect Syn.

When we get home, I get Hays cleaned up and set his nose. We have dinner and before I head off to work, I take the boys out back to run some drills to prepare them for hockey practice starting after the Labor Day holiday.

Lorelei works weekends and I have them off. She's a bartender at an uppity bar. They pay her a good hourly wage, and she makes really nice tips. I don't have to worry about her, but she has been acting weird herself lately. After I run a couple drills with the boys, I move to the deck and sit in one of the Adirondack chairs next to my sister. She takes a long drink from the glass of clear liquid in her hand.

"Is that water or vodka?" I joke with her.

"Not drinking." She doesn't say more as she continues to look off at the bay in the distance.

"You going to tell me what's eating at you?"

"Nope. Who are you working with tonight?"

"JD, as always." I chuckle. She knows this. JD and I have been partners for two years and friends for longer.

"Who is Karston's partner now that his girlfriend is on maternity leave?" Her words are said quietly, but I still turn to look at her. She has a look like she sucked on a lemon.

"Karston wasn't dating Jas. He thought of her as an annoying little sister. Why?"

She calms but only slightly. "He was always running off to take care of her."

"Not really. We all helped Jas because, like me, she was a single parent until she got with Ryan."

"She didn't have kids until she got with her doctor husband."

"Her little brother and sister are practically her kids since she's been raising them. I've told you several times you need to come to the company picnics so you can meet her. You'd like her. She's a lot like you in some ways."

I chuckle and get up from my chair. "There is a party on Monday. Come with us?"

"Fine. If I must." She huffs and stands too. "Get your

ass to work before JD makes decisions without you." Her laugh settles me, and I don't question her further about her interest in Karston.

"What's eating at you?" JD's voice breaks me from my thoughts as I stare out the window of the ambulance.

"Nothing."

"That's not what I heard."

I turn to look at him. His extremely blue eyes look stark against his darker skin tone and are focused on me as he turns from the road for a moment. My eyes are an ice blue, but his are brighter than mine and the girls fall at his feet for them.

"What did you hear?" I grit my teeth. We've been on shift for almost six hours, and I know I've been grumpier than normal. He and I are usually joking around, but currently I have an attitude like Karston, the old man of our midnight's group. He's always in a bad mood, but lately he's been worse. I guess I'm contending with him currently. I can't keep Syn out of my head. If I can't get her to be exclusive and under contract with me on Tuesday, I don't know what I'm willing to do. Sacrifice my membership? Maybe.

"I heard from Boz that you walked some hottie out of the club the other night."

Most of the club stuff is exclusive and not shared, but Boz, JD, and I have known each other since peewee hockey. There are very few secrets between the three of us. Boz won't give names just gossip, such as this. He saw me with a hottie. The biggest nugget of information here is the fact I walked her out. JD knows the significance of that. He's a whip-master at the club and currently doesn't do more than whip others. He hasn't had a sub in so long or even a fuck buddy. That is one of the secrets our group has. He holds that one tight to the vest.

"Yep." I pop the *p* and turn back to looking out the window until a call comes in and we get busy. I'm not going to give him any information. I don't know what to say for the most part.

"Happy Labor Day," Jas says as she leans in to kiss my cheek. Her husband growls, and I laugh as I tease him by twisting her around and holding on to her tighter.

"Let her go, now, jerk face." His voice comes across with extra venom. He's trying to watch his cussing as he has one hand on his newborn son's car seat and the other holding on to Jas's little seven-year-old sister, Raqi.

"Just kidding, Ryan." I chuckle again and swing toward my sister. "This is my sister, Lorelei." I introduce her, and she reaches out and shakes hands with Jasmin and Ryan. "You know the gang." I wave to my boys. All of them are on their cells, and I hate that they have them. "Boys, rules." I remind them that they can't be on them.

"But, Dad, Bas is asking about fun things to do today. His mom has no clue," Hays complains.

"You know the rules, bud."

"Fine. Hey, Jasmin." He waves at her.

"Hey, kiddo, how's hockey?" she asks all three of them.

"Practice for us starts tomorrow," Dyne offers before he smacks Hays on the shoulder, and they take off across the park. JD and Karston move to stand with us. All four of us have been a team for a while now. With Jasmin on maternity leave, it's strange not to have her working with us.

Every year Eastport Ambulance Service has an end of the summer picnic on Labor Day. This year they are having it at Eastport Park.

"Congratulations on the new baby. May I see?" Lorelei asks as she looks toward the baby seat. Jasmin goes to grab him from Ryan.

"Let me. You shouldn't be lifting anything." He turns the carrier around and we all look into the baby seat.

"He's a cutie. Can't decide who he looks more like though. By the way, you look good for just having him." Lorelei waves a hand up and down Jasmin's body. Jas normally would be wearing dark Gothic sexy clothes, but she's dressed in a T-shirt and a pair of denim shorts that look like the edges were cut instead of bought. It's different and takes me aback for a moment. I wonder if her husband finally got his way with her dress.

"Thank you. I feel like I can't get enough sleep, even though Ryan is constantly helping. And I can't wait until I can fit in my normal clothes again. I'm between maternity and regular sizes. Oh, and don't get me started on nursing." She laughs. "Come on, let's go sit down. I thought you were a figment of your brother's imagination until now. I want all the tea on him." Jas takes Lorelei's hand and moves toward the picnic tables. I notice that Ryan must have brought a nicer chair for Jas to sit in.

"Well, Ryan, when you gonna let me have my partner back?" Karston asks in his scratchy voice. He moved here from Texas and has a touch of a Southern accent.

"Not sure. She wants to continue one night a week, but we'll have to see how Grant takes to bottles too. Then there's Leif bugging for her to come back to the shop. He dropped off some books yesterday for her to go over."

"How are you doing?" I thump him on the back.

We all didn't approve of Ryan when he first wanted to get with Jas, not only because of the age difference between them but because he's a doctor. A doctor who Karston had found out was a nurse chaser until he saw Jasmin at the club. But when Ryan proved he only wanted to protect and take care of her, we couldn't stop him. He even helps with her siblings.

# Chapter Five

EMERSYN

Tonight was the first hockey practice, and no matter how much I wanted to be there I couldn't because I had a surgery go late. I can't wait to go to the club later. I haven't been able to get Trevor out of my mind. I've decided that if he asks again to be on contract, I'm going for it.

I've never been in a contracted relationship before. This could be a good change. It doesn't mean he and I are in a relationship outside the club. I would continue to hide my real life from him. I don't want my two lives to interact. I've spent too long keeping them separate, and I plan to keep doing that.

After dinner with my mom and Bas, I'm in my room getting ready. I think next week I'll contact my realtor and tell her I'm ready to start looking at houses. My hair is hanging loose again down my back. I wear it up so much during the week that I can't stand to have it up when I'm off work. I know Trevor likes it braided, so I have a ponytail holder with me.

This time I'm dressed in a black floral lace minidress and a black thong. The dress has a matching choker in lace, but I'm not wearing it because I don't want him to think I'm under contract with anyone but him. I slip on a pair of black sky-high fuck me heels in the hope he does just that in them, like he did with my boots last time. I grab my trench coat and a black mask from the drawer where I hide them from Bas. My mother knows what I do, and she has no judgement. I step out into the main living room, where she is seated on the sofa watching reruns of *Downton Abbey*.

"Are you out of here?" She takes me in and shakes her head. "What kind of eye makeup do you call that?" She waves a hand at me.

"It's a modified siren eye." I preen and make her laugh. "Don't you like it?"

"It's a bit strange, but it makes your eyes look big. You're beautiful, as always." She moves toward me and takes me in her arms for a hug. "I won't wait up."

I smile down at her. Normally, without heels on, I'm only an inch taller than her. Her Italian and Greek roots are where I get my olive complexion from. My dark thick hair I got from my father. He was Polynesian. He came to the mainland for medical school and fell in love with my momma.

"Go celebrate your win tonight," my mother says and returns to the sofa.

"Thank you. Love you." I move toward the door. For the first time in five years, I didn't have to write a check to my ex-husband. It's a win I've been waiting for. I also got sole, physical custody of Bas. If Caleb wants to see him, he has to come here and only under supervision until he tells the courts what happened. Bas won't talk about it. That's the other thing I accomplished today, Bas starts counseling in a couple of weeks.

"There are several moms at hockey practice you probably won't like, but I made sure to let them know you weren't interested in any of the single dads." She laughs as I head out the door. She knows me so well.

After the divorce, she tried to get me to date. But after everything Caleb put me through, I wasn't interested in dating. He messed with my head and my pocketbook. I wasn't going to let another man do that to me. Most men see me as a surgeon and because of my family's money think they'll get a share of that too. I learned my lesson with Caleb. Prenups are our friends. I won't ever marry again, and if for some reason I decide to be stupid, I'll make them sign a prenuptial agreement. As I'm thinking that, an image of Trevor flashes across my mind. I shake my head and step off the elevator and make my way to my car.

Arriving at the club a short while later, I slip the mask over my face and make sure my ID is locked in the glove box before exiting my vehicle. I like that I don't have to worry about carrying money or credit cards while here. I don't know where I'd put it in my outfit for one thing. And two, I wouldn't want my purse left somewhere and someone find it. When I check in, they use a PIN code to confirm my identity.

The same large security guard from last week greets me at the door before letting me in. The hostess checks me in after I enter my PIN code on the pad. I'm more nervous tonight than I was last week as I hand my jacket over to the coat attendant. I don't know if it's because I've made a decision regarding Trevor, or because of the outfit I wore tonight. My dress is so sheer it is definitely see-through. The floral designs are strategically placed across my breasts and thong over my pussy. My ass cheeks are in full view under the lace. As soon as the door opens, Trevor is waiting there. He looks me up and down and shakes his head.

"I thought it was all in my imagination how sexy you were, but I was wrong, you're so much more." He reaches out and moves with me to the bar area.

"How did you know I was here?"

"I guessed," he says, not looking at me.

"Boz told you?" I remember the guard texting on his phone.

"Yeah. I hope you don't mind. I needed to know what your answer was going to be."

"Yes, Sir." I drop my eyes, and he lifts my chin to look at me.

"Are you serious?"

"Yes." I smile from behind my mask, and he pulls me into his arms and kisses my forehead. I didn't think a fore-head kiss could be as intimate as a kiss on the mouth, but his kisses are. My knees almost buckle every time he does it. Just like him, I thought my imagination was playing tricks on me. But he's as hot as I remember.

Tonight he's in black jeans and another black shirt that buttons up. This one is silky looking. His dark hair is again brushed up into a type of faux hawk style. His ice-blue eyes are staring into mine, and I can't help it when I have to lower my lids so he doesn't see how excited I am to see him.

Maybe he could be the reason I change my rules.

Once we are seated at the table, he shows me that he got me a glass of white wine. I take a sip and am shocked that it's a Pinot Grigio. It's what I ordered last time.

"Shall we?" He waves his hand to the tablet.

"Yes. I'm in a mood to celebrate and blow some energy." I smile, giving him more information than I should.

"Celebrate? What are we celebrating, my Syn?" He holds up his beer bottle to tap my wine glass.

"I got rid of some excess baggage." I pause for a moment, wanting to give him more, but I don't. I cannot believe I contemplated telling him more.

I reach for the tablet and log in, then move to the contracts tab. I fill in the necessary information and make sure I add the clause about us not having relations outside the club. I also include that we aren't to identify the other if we see each other outside of here. I have to have that protection for my family and job.

When I hand the tablet to him, he looks it over and puts his thumb to it as way of signature. Either one of us can terminate the contract at any time without any reason.

We sit for a bit and finish our drinks, but I can tell he's not happy.

"Trevor?" I don't know what more to ask him, so I just say his name. I trust him not to hurt me, but I need to know what is going on behind those sharp eyes.

"Syn, I would never out you." He leans forward and takes my hands. He looks them over.

Trevor

Her hands are so beautiful. I imagine she's a piano player by how delicate yet strong they are. Her skin is smooth. I look up and down her sexy body behind the sheer gown she's wearing. I love that she doesn't dress in leather or costumes. Instead, she wears what she would to bed with me.

I signed the contract, but I didn't want to. I wanted to demand that we go out outside this club. It is something we are going to have to work up, just like the kissing. She continues to bite those sexy, full lips of hers, and I can't take it anymore.

"Syn, let's go to my room, where we can talk." I stand and pull her up with me. We make our way to my room, just like we did last week. I unlock the door and direct her to enter.

I need to get her out of her head and off kilter.

"Strip. Shoes too. Present on the table." I point to the

spanking bench in the corner. She turns to look at me with a question in her eyes. "Oh, my little Syn, we are going to talk. Now listen or I'll give you five."

She slips her heels off, and I watch as she drops down to a very petite five-foot-four height. She is almost a foot shorter than me. She reaches into her cleavage and pulls out a hair tie. She braids her hair into a long plait over her shoulder. She then slips her thong down her shapely legs. I move across the room and remove my shirt and belt. My boots come off and I unbutton my jeans. I grab the flogger from the wall and slip a condom into my back pocket.

The sight that greets me when I turn around is the sexiest thing I've seen. She's lying on her stomach. Her feet are lined up with the legs of the bench. Her arms are stretched over her head, and her face is turned toward me. Her liquid green eyes that remind me of cat's eye marbles are watching everything I'm doing. Her olive-colored ass is on display along with the thin strip of hair she has at her pussy lips. She fidgets as I slap the flogger against my hand, the strands of it swish through the air before they make contact with my palm. I set the flogger next to her face and move to the front legs of the bench. After I pull up the cuffs and wrap them around each wrist, I move to the back and secure her legs. As I strap her in, I watch her body for signs of distress. If anything, she's getting more and more turned on.

I pick up the flogger and drag it down her beautiful back. I take in the sexy tattoo along her side and down her hip to her thigh. I'd noticed it before but forgot how much it turned me on to see it all. Her breathing increases as I continue to slide the flogger up and down her body. I notice she's up on her toes, and I leave her for a moment to get the bench attachment for shorter women.

"I want to take care of you, Syn." My voice is husky and full of emotion as I rest her feet on the bar.

"I can't, Sir," she answers me.

"Why not?"

When she doesn't respond, I pull the flogger back and slap it against the flesh across her ass. She moans and strains against her cuffs.

"Tell me," I demand.

"I don't trust men outside this environment," she confesses, and I slide a finger along her soaked core. Her clit is erect and begging for attention. I can smell her desire and want to give her more, but I instead move around and gently slap her flesh with the flogger, bringing a flush to it. The pink under her olive skin turns me on. Her coloring is so exotic.

"What nationality are you?" I couldn't stop the personal question from leaving my lips if I wanted to.

"My mother is Greek and Italian. My father was Polynesian." She doesn't hesitate to tell me that, but she won't tell me more about herself. Granted, I haven't pushed hard, but I can see her hiding behind that mask. I want to see all of her face. Until that moment, I know she won't give me more of herself.

"I wanted to take you to dinner sometime. You trust me here but not outside these doors?"

"I can't talk about it."

I can't push her emotionally, but I will push her physically by continuing to whip her body. The strands of leather are soft and don't break her skin. They just bring blood to the surface. When I get to her ass, I give a bit more of a snap to the flogger and see the small, thin welts that will fade quickly against her skin. I step away and retrieve a vibrator as her body that was on the brink of orgasm comes down. I like using vibrators on her. From what I've seen so far, they take her over the top. As soon as I'm behind her, I lubricate the vibrator and rub it along her rosebud. She presses back, and I push the vibrator into her. I slowly push it in and out of her body as I pick up the flogger and drag it across her skin again.

I take her back up again, and just before she's ready to explode, I stop all action. I pull out the vibrator and set down the flogger.

"Please, Sir. Please, I need it," she begs, her voice cracking.

My palm slaps down on her fuller ass cheek. I keep my hand pressed there for a moment and then pull it back to see the pink mark against her flesh. She moans and begs again.

"You better stay quiet, little sub, or I'm going to stuff something in that sexy mouth of yours," I growl. I'm getting close to my limit with her too. My cock is straining in my jeans. She pouts, and I unstrap her from the table. I help her up and move her to the sofa, where I push her to her knees. I pull the condom from my pocket and then drop my jeans. She keeps her eyes on floor, and I watch her body shiver when my feet enter her line of sight.

Gripping her braid, I tip her head back and push my cock toward her mouth. She opens and I fuck into her mouth over and over. Tears burst from her eyes because I'm pushing her, but I don't stop. She needs this as much as I do. When I'm about to come, I pull back and lift her up. I position her on the sofa, hanging her body over the back, her knees on the cushion. With the condom on, I grab her braid and slam into her tight body.

"Yes, Sir!" she cries out, and I groan from being here again. I fuck into her over and over. When she's there at the precipice again, I pull out and flip us around so I'm seated and she's straddling my lap. She slides down my length and starts riding me. I bite her neck and drag my beard against her skin. I take a nipple into my mouth while squeezing the other.

"Come, Syn," I order her, and she slams down on me again and again before she stops and throws her head back. I grip her small waist and move her a couple more times before I explode in the condom. I empty everything into it. She screams again before she falls to my chest. Both of us are out of breath. I lift her up to pinch off the condom and drop it into the trash next to the sofa. I move her so she's sitting sideways on my lap, then I wrap around her body and hold her while she comes down. When she's settled, I offer her the water I left by the sofa. After she takes small sips, her head falls back and she looks at me. Her beautiful, expressive hazel eyes watch me from behind her mask.

"Why do you push me?" Her voice is soft and drowsy sounding.

I stand and carry her to the satin covered bed. I lie down with her facing me and hold her.

"Sleep if you need to."

"I can't. I have to get back home."

"Is there someone waiting for you?" I hate that I asked, but a piece of me needs to know.

"It's just getting late, and I work tomorrow." She moves away, not giving me the answer I need.

# Chapter Six

EMERSYN

I'm moving through my office in frustration. I dial my mother's number as I walk down the hallway to the elevator.

"Mom, I'm not going to make it again."

In the month since Bas has been in hockey, I've missed every one of his games. He's not upset. He tells me all the time he's proud of me for helping other kids, but I know it has to hurt. It's been a busy month between football and hockey both going strong and now cross country running. I'm one of the few pediatric orthopedic specialists in town. The others work with adults mostly but will help me so I'm not on call all the time.

I finally had a chance to make this scrimmage. It isn't an official game, but still I planned to be there. And now I'm being paged to the ER.

"It's okay, Emmy. There was a bad injury. It's Bas's

friend. They called the scrimmage. After he showers, he wants to come to the hospital and check on him. Can he?"

"Sure. We can get dinner." I don't say why I've been delayed. I've been called in to consult. It could be this kid, but I don't know yet.

I step onto the elevator and take it down to the first floor.

Trevor and I have been meeting up regularly every Tuesday night for the last month. I've never been so well taken care of sexually. He is constantly pushing me. He still won't tell me why he does it, but I love it.

I step into the ER. Dr. Richards, my friend who helped me get this job, is still on paternity leave as his wife had their baby at the end of August. He will be back soon though. I approach the nurses' station and observe Dr. McKay standing there looking at X-rays.

"What you got, Sawyer?" I step up and look at them with him.

"Hey, Emersyn, thanks for coming down. I'm not sure what we got here. It appears to be a possible MCL tear. Would you take a look?"

"Of course. Which room?" He points to a room across from where we're standing. I grab the chart and head that way.

"Hello, Hayden Myer, I'm Dr. St. James." I look up from the chart when I hear the gasps. "Oh, hello you."

"You're Bas's mom," two identical voices say, and I smile at them.

"I am. Tell me what happened." I step over to the

beautiful woman who looks too young to be their mother. "You must be Mrs. Myer. My son got in trouble with yours in August."

"Oh, I'm not his mom. I'm Miss Myer. They're my nephews. His dad and other brother should be here shortly."

"Do you have medical consent?" I flip through the chart to look, and I see the consent on file.

"Yeah."

"Okay. So tell me, Hayden." I give the boy my full attention. He tells me that the same boy who beat him up in August checked him into the boards. I know that in their age group checking isn't allowed. "Mind if I flex it and check it over."

"No."

He cringes when I touch him. His knee is already swollen. I carefully palpate and flex it around. It has a slight give when I do a lateral shift. When I flex the knee into ninety degrees, I carefully twist his foot and see him cringe.

"I need to order an MRI."

"What's that?" the other twin asks.

"What's your name?"

He pushes his shoulders back before answering. "I'm Holdyn, with a *y*, but you can call me Dyne."

I smile at him. "Want to know a secret?" I lean toward him.

He nods and his brother leans toward us.

"I want to know too."

"I'm Emersyn with a *y*." I chuckle.

"Dad, did you hear that?" Dyne says as he looks over my shoulder.

I turn and stop dead in my tracks.

"Syn?" he says my name, and I feel the flush hit my skin. All he has to do is talk to me and he's got me ready for him, even in my real life. This can't happen.

Oh. My. God.

"Shit," I say softly but not soft enough as a bigger boy next to Trevor smiles.

"Mr. Myer, can we talk?" I move toward him, needing to tell him he has to have another doctor look after his son.

"You were going to tell us what the test you want to do is." Hayden stops me. "I have a *y* in my name too." I swing back around. I'm not going to take it out on these sweet boys.

"You're right, Hayden. Do you have a nickname?"

Trevor moves in behind me, and I try not to get distracted from what I'm supposed to be doing.

"They call me Hays."

"I like that. An MRI is a magnetic resonance imaging test. I need to see if you tore a ligament in your knee. The X-rays Dr. McKay took showed no broken bones."

"Will it hurt?"

I move to his bed and sit next to his hip, taking his hand in mine. His twin moves closer to me, and I hold on to his shoulder with my other hand.

"No, it won't hurt. You'll lie down on a bed and it will move into a big tunnel that will take pictures."

"Hays doesn't go anywhere without me," Dyne adds.

"Holdyn, he's going to have to go by himself. I might be able to go with him, but you won't be able to." Trevor's deep voice comes from behind me, and I can't stop the shiver that runs over my body. He touches my shoulder and I almost jump over the bed to get away from him. He can't do this. Our contract says we aren't supposed to acknowledge each other, and he just violated that.

"How about this, Dyne, I'll go with him. I'll be in the room right outside the MRI with the techs? I'll take care of him for you. Sound good?"

"You promise you won't leave him?" Dyne's voice cracks with his ten-year-old youth.

"He won't see me, but he'll have headphones on and can hear me. I promise."

"What do you say, Hays?" Dyne and his twin look at each other and talk in that silent twin talk I've heard so much about. Finally, Hays nods, and I stand up.

"Okay, I'll get it ordered."

I move from the room with Trevor following behind me. His hand is at the small of my back, and I can feel the heat of it through my clothes and lab coat.

Gritting my teeth, I turn my head slightly. "Let me go now, Trevor." His hand drops, and I move to the sink to wash my hands. "You are supposed to ignore me," I tell him. "I'll go with him to MRI, but I won't be able to treat him."

"Bullshit." His voice raises, and he advances on me. I look around and see we are attracting attention. I nod so that Sawyer knows I'm okay. Trevor reaches for my arm, but I step back.

"Don't touch me." My voice is laced with venom. "I won't jeopardize my license by treating your son and being what we are to each other."

He moves again and is standing over me.

"Syn, don't deny what we are. For a month we've given each other many orgasms. I've fucked you so hard I thought my eyes were going to cross, and I know yours did." His crude words cause my heart to beat faster, but I won't do that here.

"My name is *Dr.* St. James." I spit out.

"Well, Dr. St. James, Syn, what is it?"

I look around again and see my mother being directed by a nurse to Hayden's room. She looks over at me, and Bas stops when he sees the man standing over me. I watch as fear crosses his face. I won't have this affect my son.

"Red," I say, and move away from Trevor. I nod to my mother and give Bas a small smile before I go behind the nurses' station.

Trevor

For the second time she has stunned me. I was shocked to see her when she turned around in the exam room. But for her to say her safe word again while outside of the club can only mean one thing. One thing I don't want to think about right now. I move toward my son's room and see Cynthia and Bas standing there.

I met Cynthia and her grandson, Bas, at the first hockey game. It all clicks into place then. The mom who was on call. The mom who was missed but called several times and even video chatted with him before a game. The mom I haven't met. My Syn is actually Emersyn St. James. Dr. Emersyn St. James, the new pediatric orthopedic surgeon. I've heard many stories about her but haven't gotten to meet her in person, or so I thought I hadn't.

"Why were you mad at my mom?" Bas asks me, and I see her in his eyes. I see the nose and fuller lips. Shit.

"I wasn't mad at your mom. We were discussing what they are going to do with Hays," I lie, and he knows it.

"My dad used to stand over her like that. He said he'd hurt her." He drops the bomb in the room and Cynthia pauses.

"Sebastian, what did you say?"

"He said he'd hurt her. I told him he couldn't, so he pushed me. He told me that if I thought I was man enough to dish it out, I was man enough to take it." His voice is quiet but loud enough for his mother to hear.

"Bas, that's what happened?" Emersyn moves toward him. I smell her spring floral scent as she moves past me and takes her son in her arms.

"Mom, not in front of the guys." Bas pulls away, and I cover my smile by pulling my lips in.

"They're ready for you now, Hays." A tech steps into the room pushing a wheelchair.

I lift Hays and help him into the chair, then I walk with them to the MRI room. While the techs get Hayden arranged on the table, I turn to Emersyn in the control room.

"I need you to take care of him. You're the best here." My words are just above a whisper, and I watch her full lips purse together. I want to kiss the shit out of them, but she called red and I can't do that.

"I can't be his physician and be with you." She turns to look at me, and I see the hurt in her eyes. She turns away from me.

"We are ready." The technician moves toward us. "Can you please wait in the hall, Trevor?" he asks.

I step out into the hall to wait. I don't know what to do right now. My son is hurt. He needs the best care, and that's her, but I also don't want to be without her. I come to the only decision there is.

By the time they are finished, I've paced and anxiously ran through every moment I've had with Syn. It's all I can do. My boys are my priority. She walks on the other side of the wheelchair, holding his hand. I see the slight tear tracks on his face. He's hurting, and I want to take away the pain. I've had to be both a father and mother to them all.

When we return to the room, Emersyn steps out while the tech and I get him arranged in the bed. The room is filled with both of our families. The staff usually limits the number of visitors, but because it's me they are taking that into consideration. Maybe when she's done treating him, we can figure something out. But realistically I know that isn't going to happen. I broke one of her major rules.

Emersyn steps back into the room with a nurse and Sawyer, the head of the ER and a doctor I know quite well.

"After a lot of consideration, we've come up with a plan," Sawyer says as he moves to the bed. Emersyn stays back and I look between the two of them.

"Wait." I stop Sawyer. I know he's a brilliant doctor, but right now my son needs the best in this field. "I thought Dr. St. James was treating him." My voice has a roughness to it that must be more so than normal because my family all looks at me. I'm ready to clear everyone out and demand that Emersyn do what she has to, then I'd like to spank her ass for saying red.

"I asked Dr. St. James to consult, and she's given her suggestions." Sawyer looks between the two of us, unsure of what's going on with us.

"Then I'd like to hear them from her." I cross my arms over my chest and brace my legs apart. I'm not fucking around here. "My son deserves to be treated by the best in the field, just like everyone else. I've asked that Dr. St. James stay on his case."

"Em—" Sawyer starts.

"No." My voice is a growl. Her son moves toward her, and Lorelei stands to join me along with my oldest, Brooklyn.

"Um, Dr. St. James." Sawyer tips his head toward her, and I watch her spine straighten. Under her lab coat she's in black slacks that hug her hips, and I bet her ass looks sexy as fuck in them. She has on a white button top with a gray vest over it that accentuates all her curves and makes her boobs more prominent.

"Thank you, Dr. McKay. I'll take it from here." Her voice is firm, lacking the normal sexiness that comes through it. She's angry. The little brat is going to get many deserved spankings when I get my hands on her again. She takes her beautiful eyes off me and moves to the bed, where she stands with Hayden and Holdyn.

"The MRI showed that you have a grade two tear in your MCL, your medial cruciate ligament. That's the one that stabilizes your knee side to side. When that kid checked you, he must have been in a crouched position and your knee took the brunt of the impact. Because it's only a minor tear, I'd like to do some wait and see things instead of rushing you to surgery." She turns to me. "I'd like to brace him, rest it, do some PT and observation." When she turns back to the boys, I watch as each takes a hand. She has my boys wrapped around her little finger too. Just like she has me. "You'll be on crutches for the first week, in a brace that will immobilize your knee in a straight position. I'm going to get you set up to see a physical therapist who is really good."

"Is she the same one Bas sees?" Hays asks, and I look at her son. Bas doesn't appear to have any noticeable injuries. She shakes her head as her full lips tip up into a smile.

"No, sweetie. Bas doesn't see a physical therapist."

"Of course, he does," Dyne argues with her.

"No." She looks at Bas and then back to the boys. "Bas

sees a therapist to help him deal with his father's and my divorce. She's a different kind of therapist." She points to Hays. "You'll see one who works with your knee to make it strong and help it heal."

"Oh, okay." Both of my boys nod.

The nurse hands the knee immobilizing brace to Emersyn as Sawyer excuses himself from the room. From my vantage point across from her on the other side of the bed, I can see right down Emersyn's cleavage when she leans forward to talk directly to Hays. I'm enjoying the view and miss what she says to my son. She looks up and immediately stands straight with a sour look on her face.

"Mom, Bas, please go wait in the lobby," she orders. Her mom gives her a concerned look before ushering Bas out.

"I guess Brook and I will wait in the lobby too," Lorelei says.

As soon as the curtain is closed behind Brooklyn, I turn back to Emersyn to ask what I missed. My question dies in my throat as I watch her approach Holdyn and help him pull off his hockey gear. He removes the shorts he was wearing under his pants and hands them to Hayden. She helps Holdyn redress, without the pads, and then stands there.

"Can you help me too?" Hayden asks quietly.

"I got you, buddy." I move to him.

"No, Dad. I want Emersyn to help me."

She softens instantly, and I remember seeing a similar look on her face whenever I helped her.

"Sure. But remember around other people you have to call me Dr. St. James. It isn't fair that you can call me by my name and they can't." She smiles at him and then carefully helps him into his brother's shorts. "How about your dad help me here?" she asks him as she moves to his leg. I know why she's so good at her job. It's all about the kids. She talks to them as if they matter. It's their bodies, after all.

When Hayden nods in agreement, I stand next to Emersyn. I can see the pain is really starting to get to my kid. Together we get him into the brace and it strapped on. I tried not to touch her as we worked. Every time our shoulders brushed, she'd move away. I want to touch her. I want to hold her.

"He needs to be in it at all times until he sees me next Friday. I'll walk with him to therapy, and afterward we'll determine how long he'll be in the brace. You can unstrap it to ice his knee, but don't let him move it without it on. To shower, wrap a trash bag around it. Keep it as dry as you can. No baths." She is no-nonsense and clinical with me.

"Okay, buddy." Her voice softens when she turns to Hays. "You heard what I said. Always in the brace. Use the crutches to walk, not on the bully. Okay? And ice it every few hours."

She turns back to me.

"I'm going to prescribe Tylenol with codeine for the next couple of days. Give it to him tonight, every six hours. On Monday switch to just ibuprofen."

She reaches out a hand to Hays and then Holdyn. "It was a pleasure meeting such handsome gentlemen. I have to go, but I'll see you at your first follow-up next Friday."

"Can you come check on me tomorrow and bring Bas?"

Emersyn smiles softly at him. "I can't, but thank you for the lovely invite."

I watch as she steps out of the room without a glance back. When we are finally discharged, I don't see Emersyn anywhere, nor do I see her family in the lobby. She's running from me and thinks she's going to get away, but we are going to discuss this.

# Chapter Seven

EMERSYN

All weekend I avoided talking to Trevor. He actually used his son and mine to get to me. I've been focused on dealing with Bas's revelation too. I left a message for my lawyer to call me as soon as he could. Maybe it's time I find an attorney here in Eastport.

My phone rings as I'm walking out the back of the hospital toward my car. I pull it out and see Ryan's number.

"Hello, Emmy, how is it going?"

"Good. Hey, would you ask your attorney if he could suggest a local family lawyer?"

"Is Caleb bothering you again?"

"No. Honestly, though, it's only a matter of time. But I should get one in Eastport now that I live here and the judge in Boston deferred my case to this court system. Plus, I don't want to pay my attorney's travel fees to come here." I laugh.

Distracted, I don't see the person advancing on me until they are standing right next to me. I startle and squeal into the phone.

"Emmy, are you okay?" Ryan asks, and I hold my hand to my chest.

"Yeah, sorry. Someone just startled me."

"Do you need to call security? Where are you? I have a friend I can call."

"No. It's fine. It's not him. I have to go. Text me that information, and tell Collin I said hi." I huff out a breath as I hang up the phone.

"You avoiding me, Syn?"

"Yes," I answer him honestly. After everything we've done, he deserves that. "I can't do this. I told you on Friday I wasn't going to continue our..." I pause. "I can't continue our contract if I'm treating your son." He and I were not in a relationship.

Because of me.

That thought gives me pause and I watch Trevor for a moment. I miss him. Even though we wouldn't have seen each other until tomorrow, I still miss him. I would have been anticipating our time together, but now I only have the memories of it.

He reaches for me and pulls me to him. I worry he's going to kiss me, so I reach up and cover my mouth. Without the safeguards of the contract, there is no stopping him from pushing that limit.

"I'm not going to kiss you, Emersyn. I want to talk." He releases my arms and steps back. I drop my hand and take him in completely. He's dressed in a dark navy blue EMT uniform with the Star of Life emblem on the chest. It hits me then.

"You're a paramedic." It's not a question but a statement of fact. I remember Hays saying his dad could set his nose. I also remember some of the things Trevor tried to share with me over the past month.

"My shift starts in a couple of hours, but I wanted to see you first. Emersyn, I want to see you outside of the club."

"I can't. I won't jeopardize my license for another man." I move past him, not wanting to rehash how fucked up my past was or why I can't do this anymore.

"You can treat my son. You shouldn't treat me, but you could, if you needed to. I looked it up."

"It doesn't matter. I won't do it. It's over. I had rules and you broke them. I can't trust you now."

He pulls me into his body, slamming me hard against his chest. I look up into his storm-filled eyes.

"You can always trust me. You just don't want to. I'll be waiting." He pulls away after he drops a soft kiss on my forehead.

I head home and pull into the parking garage when it hits me. I won't be seeing him ever again. I pushed him away this time. I've been holding him at arm's length for so long. I did this. He's right, I could treat his son and still be with him. I could see him outside of the club. But then the memories of how close it got with Caleb fill my mind. How he left me to take care of Sebastian. How he would show up at my clinicals and cause scenes. He once showed up drunk and threw a beer bottle at a doctor after he was asked to leave. He was upset I'd canceled his game system membership. I slide out of the car and head up to my condo.

Another week passes, and Hayden's recovery is going well. Trevor still tries to push me to see him, but I won't. I haven't been back to the club either. I don't want to play with anyone but him, and I can't do that. Just this past week Caleb left me a message at the hospital. It reminded me of why I can't do anything with Trevor.

The realtor showed me several homes over the weekend, but I didn't find one I liked. There was something wrong with each and every one of them. I'm beginning to question moving here. I know it's just because of everything that went down with Trevor. I love my job here. I've been dealing with Caleb for well over ten years, including the time we were dating. Even while we dated, I knew he wasn't the best for me. But something inside me, maybe his voice, kept telling me I wasn't good enough for anyone else.

"Mom, can I spend the night at Hays and Dyne's this weekend?" Bas asks as soon as I step into the condo. He's been bugging to visit his friends. If everything goes well this week, Hays will be out of his brace. He will, however, be sidelined from hockey for a bit longer. I'm getting him fit for a brace he can wear under his gear until his knee is strong enough.

"Give me a sec to get changed." I move to my room.

I slip off my heels and slide the zipper down my skirt, then drop it to the floor before taking off my blouse. I change into my favorite ripped up soft jeans and a baggy sweater. I step into the bathroom and look at myself critically, as I always do. Caleb's voice fills my head, criticizing everything. It hits me then. I've let my ex-husband have a say in everything in my life for over ten years. I've listened to his voice over and over. But I have found a better man. A man who wants me no matter what. A man I've pushed away.

I'm doing this. I'm going to get better, and maybe we'll see what happens.

I take my hair down and let it fall down my back. I grab my purse, a pair of socks, and a pair of mid-calf boots.

"Let's go to dinner," I holler when I exit my room.

"Pizza?" Bas asks, and I smile at him.

"Yeah, buddy, let's do a mommy and son date." I hug him to my side.

"Good. I'm going to go out with some ladies I met," Mom says, a soft look fills her face. She knows I don't normally take Bas out for pizza because I'm always dieting, but tonight I don't care. I like my body for what it is. I love who I am and what I've accomplished. I'm going to stop letting Caleb control my life.

We are sitting in the restaurant eating sausage and pepperoni pizza, Bas's favorite. He's telling me all about how the coach suspended the boy who hurt Hays. The kid will be out for a couple of weeks. The coach is also hard at work teaching the boys how to defend themselves. I like that he's being proactive, just in case a situation like this happens again. He tells me how Brooklyn, the twins' older brother, came into practice and showed them some moves. He's in a more advanced hockey program. He also tells me how school and counseling are going. It's been so long since we've done this. I love my son, and I love spending time with him, but it's very rarely just the two of us. Mom is usually present. Or I was focused on other things when we were in Boston. That's another good thing about moving here. Bas and I have developed more of a relationship. I don't have to worry about Caleb or money.

"It's Monday night, Bas, we need to get home. You have school tomorrow," I say when we finish eating.

"Mom, you didn't answer my question about this weekend."

It's dark out as we walk toward our car in the parking lot. Bas skips ahead, chattering about the twins and all the reasons I should let him go. We hit a particularly dim spot between the light poles when I'm grabbed from behind. An arm wraps around my waist and a hand covers my mouth.

"Give me the purse," a guy whispers in my ear. He pokes something into my side.

All the years I lived in Boston or visited other major cities I was never mugged. But here in Eastport I'm attacked with my son present. I uncurl my arm and let my small bag slide down. The guy yanks it, and I can't stop the cry as it pulls on my arm. Bas stops and turns. He has the car keys in his hand, and I pray he stays put.

"Tell the kid to come here."

I shake my head hard. My eyes fix on Bas, hoping he gets the message to stay put. The guy pulls his hand from my waist and slams it into my kidney. I scream behind his hand when something sharp pricks my skin through my sweater. He has a knife. He didn't stab me. The blade nicked me when he turned it from me. He's not trying to kill me, just steal my money.

His hand slips from my mouth. "Bas, stay there," I order, and the guy hits me again. This time the blade digs a bit deeper. "Please take my purse. There's money in it. Just don't hurt my son."

"Tell him to come here."

I don't know what he wants with Bas. For a second I think it might be Caleb, but I don't recognize the voice.

"Sebastian," I say his name softly, and wait until I have his full attention. "Run," I yell and rear back my head.

The knife presses into me, but the guy pulls away and throws me to the ground. I hear a horn honking and the pounding of Bas's feet as he runs. The man kicks me in the ribs and tries to stomp on me, but I roll away.

"Bitch," he says, and takes off running. "I'll get you," he yells as he disappears into the darkness.

I can't lie here. I need to make sure my son is okay. I push up onto my hands and knees. My ribs pull and warm blood drips down my back. I get to my feet and scour the area for Bas.

"Bas," I scream his name. Please don't let him be hurt.

"Mommy."

I hear his voice and turn to see him with the hostess from the pizza parlor. I stumble to him and keep myself on my feet until the police and ambulance show up.

I say another silent prayer that it's not Trevor. I don't know how he'd react to this.

An hour later I'm in the ER with my mom sitting in a chair next to the bed. Bas is in the bed with me. His little body is trembling as he sleeps wrapped around me.

"Emersyn." Trevor's voice does things to me, and I instantly start crying.

Bas wakes and sees Trevor standing in the curtained opening. My son jumps up into his arms when he approaches the bed. It makes my tears come harder watching Bas take comfort from him.

"Trevor," I sob.

Trevor

I was sitting in the paramedic lounge when I overheard the nurses talking about a doctor from the hospital being attacked and mugged. As soon as they said her young son had been with her, I just knew. I was up and moving.

"Trevor, stop." Ryan reaches for me, but I push past him. He and I are about the same height, but I have more muscle on him. "She doesn't want to be disturbed," he says as I rip the curtains back.

What I see causes every muscle in my body to tremble in anger. I want to kill the fucker who hurt her. She's in a gown and the collar slips as she sits up, revealing the bruising on her upper chest. She grabs her right side, and I zone in on that when Bas jumps at me.

"I tried to save her. I pushed the panic alarm on the keys and ran, but I wanted to fight," he sobs into my chest. I wrap my arms around him, holding his body. This is the most emotion he's ever shown me. When he hangs out with the boys at practice, he'll shake my hand and say very few words to me, even after what happened with Hays. But right here in this moment he needs me, so I give him my strength as I look over his head at Emersyn. She leans back in the bed with tears running down her face.

"Emmy, honey," her mom starts but stops when I move to Emersyn's side.

Bas lets me go and carefully crawls over his mom to her other side. I lean down and kiss her forehead. She sighs, and I itch to kiss her deeply and show her how much I've missed her. It's been almost two weeks since I last had her and a week since she broke it off with me.

"How bad? What happened?" I hear how gravelly my voice is, but I can't hide it. I'm scared to touch her. She has a bruise on her cheek and mud in her hair. Again, I want to kill whoever is responsible for hurting her.

"He jumped us when we left the pizza parlor. I don't know who he was, and I didn't see his face," she says with a tremble in her voice. I brush my hand gently down her cheek over the bruise.

"I saw him, but I don't know him. He stabbed her." He points to her right side near where he's lying.

"Bas, honey, how about you and I go get some candy from the vending machine," Cynthia says, but he shakes his head.

Emersyn looks down at him and then to me. "Bas, go help Grammy get me a snack."

"Okay, Mom." He slides from the bed. "Don't leave until I come back. She needs to be protected," he says to me before exiting the curtain.

As soon as they are gone, I lean my forehead to hers. "Emmy, baby, what the fuck? You could have been killed. Please give me another chance. I can't do this anymore. I miss you," I beg her.

"I can't," she says, and sobs. "I can't put your family in danger if Caleb is behind this. He's never resorted to hurting me, but I didn't think he'd ever hurt Bas either. The man said he would get me when he ran off. I can't, Trevor." She continues to cry.

I wrap her in my arms as I sit on the bed facing her, our hips next to each other. I hold her to me until she quiets down.

"Emmy?" Ryan says from the entrance, and we both

turn to him. "Are you sure this isn't Caleb?" He knows more about her ex than I do. I want to be jealous, but I can't be.

"I'm..." She pauses. "He called the other day. Here at the office. Told me he would get what he was due."

I grit my teeth and look down at her. "Baby."

"It could be him."

"The police would like to question you again," he says, and waves for me to come with him.

"I promised Bas I wouldn't leave her side," I tell him, and he nods. I stand there while she gives the police another statement. She looks at me as she starts talking.

"My ex-husband is mad his alimony ended. He is also upset he didn't get more of my inheritance. He's been trying since our marriage to get access to it." Her eyes drop for a moment and then she looks up at me again. I know she doesn't want to reveal what she's about to say next. I squeeze her hand to let her know I'm here for her.

"Before we got married, he insisted that I have Sebastian when I got pregnant. I'd been thinking of other options because I was in medical school at the time. After Bas was born, I found out Caleb wanted me to have him because he thought it would get him into my trust fund easier. He left us when Bas was six months old. We ended up getting divorced after Bas turned five."

She takes a deep breath. "I had a good attorney but not as ruthless as his. I ended up having to pay him alimony for five years, which just ended. I also had to pay him child support for the two nights a month he had Bas. That ended before we moved here because he stopped seeing Bas after a situation happened."

"What situation?" one of the cops asks.

"I recently learned Caleb pushed Sebastian around. He didn't hit him, just kept pushing him." She fidgets with her hands for a moment. "I have a new attorney here in Eastport, and she had Caleb served at his parents' home with a restraining protective order for Bas. I know it wasn't Caleb who attacked me, but that's not to say it wasn't someone he knew or hired."

"He's done that in the past?" the cop asks.

Emersyn looks up at him and then to his partner. I want her eyes back on me when her tears start to flow. I want to comfort and shield her. She looks around the cops toward the curtain and sees Ryan standing there. He moves into the room.

"I told your mom to wait in the lobby with Bas." He doesn't leave, and I'm about to ask him to. "If you are talking about her ex, you should know he threatened me. He has a temper. He hurt Emmy emotionally, not physically. It was always her fault. He accused her of cheating numerous times." He looks to me and back to her before returning his attention to the cops. "He hired a man to break into Emmy's place in Chicago one time. Stole all her money and tore up her clothes and things."

I see red and I move without thought. "Were you with Emersyn?"

Ryan turns to me with shocked eyes. "Hell no." He shakes his head. He looks at Emersyn in the bed and something passes across his vision. "She's my friend." He emphasizes the last word. "Been for a long time. I wouldn't do that with her, not that she isn't sexy and doesn't deserve someone to be into her. But she's... She's like a little sister to me. I was there to help her after that happened." He looks behind him to see if anyone is close by. "Besides, her father was my mentor and Bas is special to me." I can tell there is more to what he's saying.

"I thought you were from Chicago," I say to Ryan. "And you from Boston." I look at Emersyn. The implications keep working around in my head as I shift my focus between the two of them.

"I was born in Chicago," she says so quietly that I almost don't hear her. I move back to her and wait for her to continue, but she doesn't.

"Okay, Emersyn, I have your discharge ready." Another physician steps into the room, and I look between Ryan and her again.

"I'm going to go home and get some sleep." She moves off the bed and heads toward the bathroom.

"Are you going to tell me what's going on?" I swing on Ryan. The cops move toward us.

"If Emmy doesn't want you to know, then no." He shakes his head. "I won't do that to her."

"What about your wife? Did you move your ex-lover here so you could start back up with her? I heard what you were like before you came here."

His fist cracks against my jaw and my head snaps back.

"Ryan, no," Emersyn screams, and the cops are on me. I turn to look at her and see she has tears in her eyes again.

"You don't understand. It's not our secret to tell. I'd never sleep with him. I love him but not in the way you think." She moves out of the room, and I watch her leave.

"What did she mean?" I turn back to Ryan, who's shaking his fist.

"Fucker, you have a hard jaw. By the way, you just completely fucked up. My wife knows Emmy and I are close. I'm faithful to my wife. But don't ever say shit like that about Emmy. You don't deserve her." He turns and walks out, and I storm off toward the ambulance bay as my radio goes off.

# Chapter Eight

## EMERSYN

I miss Trevor, but I won't be with someone who thinks that of me. Not again. Caleb had thought Ryan and I were lovers too. I've never thought that way of Ryan. He's been my best friend. He's been there with me for so much. He and my mom were there the day my world fell apart. The day my father died and the day my son came into my life. Shit, even Caleb was out smoking instead of being in the room when our son was born.

I pull up to the tattoo shop and slide out of my car. The police haven't found the guy who attacked me. They haven't found Caleb either. I'm missing going to the club. It's been three weeks since I had that kind of release. Ryan suggested I come here. I know why. He wants me to get to know Jas, and I guess it's time.

Yesterday I got to see Bailey. She's out of her cast and in physical therapy to help her build her muscles. She said she and her mother like their new apartment. But something was off with her mom. She didn't want to talk much, and I pray she isn't contemplating going back to her ex who hurt her and her daughter.

I step through the door and the buzzer goes off, letting them know I'm here. A beautiful woman with dark hair moves from the back. She's in a pair of fake leather maternity pants, a sheer top that shows off her baby bump, and a short leather bolero jacket covering her breasts. Super high-heeled boots adorn her feet. A sexy looking blond follows behind her in a suit. The man is large and looks like he could be an actor on the TV show *Vikings*.

"Princess, I wish you'd stop wearing the heels already." He's walking behind her like he's afraid she's going to fall over or trip.

It's then that Jasmin walks out. Her hair is up in cute buns. She's in a schoolgirl uniform skirt, tall thigh-high boots, and a button-down shirt with a plaid vest over it. Her shirt is opened at the collar, showing her cleavage. I can't hide my grin. This is Ryan's wife. Serves his ass right.

A laugh leaves me and both women look in my direction. They smile at me, but the guy must think I'm laughing at him. "It's not funny. She could hurt herself or the baby," he growls, and I reach up to brush the tears from my eyes.

"I'm so sorry. I was just thinking you are perfect for Ryan." I wave my hand at Jasmin. "You're beautiful and probably drive him crazy in your outfit. When I was in high school, I tried for a grunge phase and he went out of his mind." I start laughing again.

"He told me." She laughs, and I'm so glad she understands. "You two were pretty close," she says as she moves toward me.

I pull her into my body and hug her. "Congratulations. I can't wait to see the little man." My voice is soft, and I hope she knows how happy I truly am. I haven't gone to see him yet because I've been trying to keep my distance. I didn't want people to start the rumors again. Ryan and I have faced them for years.

"Come by for dinner, bring Bas. Ryan can't stop talking about him," she says, and I smile at her before turning to her friend.

"You must be Erika." I hold out my hand to her.

She looks down at my hand and cocks her head to the side, her hip popping out. "Only shake my hand if you've never slept with Ryan. If Jas won't ask, I will." Her voice has some grit to it and a slight accent.

"Nope. Ew." I don't explain more as I take her hand and shake it.

"Cool. So, what are you thinking of getting." She smiles at me and shrugs her shoulders at Jas. "Can't blame me for asking."

The big guy holds out his hand to me. "Grayson." His voice is gruff, but not like Trevor's. I miss him. But for his family's safety and the fact he hurt me, I won't go there. Her question brings him up though. The memories of all his new school comic art on his body makes me want to get something like that, but I don't.

"I'm thinking of getting a rose on my forearm with the

word 'family' in the stem." I don't explain why because I'm not ready to share how much I miss my dad. How much my family means to me.

"Let's get started."

I pull off my jacket and scarf. I'm not wearing it for warmth but decoration. My shell top is perfect for doing the forearm tattoo.

"So, what was Ryan like growing up?" Jas asks as soon as I'm seated.

"He was determined to be more than his father. To be a better doctor and to step out of that shadow. My dad used to say one day Ryan was going to realize he didn't have to be so serious and would excel then." The memory causes my chest to ache.

"Your dad and his father were friends?"

"No, they hated each other with a passion. We moved to Boston right before my dad died. My mom thinks if we'd left Chicago sooner and got away from Brent, he'd still be alive."

"Who's Brent?" Erika asks, and I look between her and Jasmin.

"That was Ryan's father," I answer.

"How did your parents meet?" Jas asks.

I smile and look down at what Erika is doing. I tell her what I told Trevor all those weeks ago.

"I miss my parents too," she says when I'm done, and I reach out with my other hand to pat hers.

"Ryan told me. He also told me how much you pushed against him about being in a relationship." I chuckle.

"Like you with Trevor," she quips back, and my smile fades.

"My ex was an asshole. I don't want to go through that again. I don't have the energy for it."

"Trevor doesn't play games. You're the first girl he's been with for longer than a night since I've known him." She pats my hand this time.

"He drives me crazy." I decide I really do need to talk to someone about him. "He thinks Ryan and I have slept together. Doesn't trust me or what we told him." I pause and bite my lip. "But Bas cares about him. I've never seen Bas like that with anyone. Well, other than Ryan."

"Men can be stupid sometimes," Erika adds as she looks up at her husband, who is seated at the counter with a laptop. He looks up with a bashful smile. "Mine decided to hide the fact he was the owner of a casino."

"Still got you in the end." He chuckles.

"I lied to Ryan about my siblings."

"You got him in the end," Erika says. "He had you collared and a ring on your finger before you could say 'What.'" She laughs.

"Well, yours married you within forty-eight hours." Jasmin flips her hand out, and I look at the necklace she's wearing. It is a collar. Then I see the one around Erika's neck. They both catch me looking.

"You want one, don't you?" Jasmin asks.

"No."

“Me thinks the lady doth protest too much.” Erika laughs harder.

“I’m serious. I don’t need one. I have Bas and my life at the hospital. I’m still trying to find a house. Man, I saw the perfect one as I was out driving around over the weekend. It was so beautiful, but it wasn’t for sale.”

“Where was it?” Jasmin asks, and I tell her.

“Wow, that’s really close to my house and not far from —” She stops and smacks her hand over her mouth. “Ryan was saying we should come to one of Bas’s hockey games. When is his next one?”

“Saturday.” I tell her the time, ignoring the fact she changed the subject. We make plans to meet up there.

Trevor

As I sit in the arena, I’m trying to prepare myself to see Emersyn again. Every weekend I see her, and every time it gets worse. She sits all the way on the opposite side of the ice so she doesn’t have to sit near us.

“Let’s sit over here.” I hear Jasmin’s voice and look down to see her leading Ryan, Emersyn, and Cynthia all in.

They sit down a section over from us. Ryan gives me the stink eye, but I’m openly staring at my girl. She’s so beautiful. Her long thick hair is in waves down her back. She’s wearing her glasses today instead of contacts. She’s in skintight black jeans and tall knee boots. Her tan top has long sleeves and a zipper pulled down from her collar to well between the swell of her breasts. My mouth waters wanting them. She sits down and Jasmin sits next to her. They are laughing and chatting. Ryan sits behind them with Cynthia next to him and his little boy in his car seat between them. Cynthia is cooing over the baby. A few minutes later the doors open again and Koda steps in with Raqi running beside him. He got his license a few weeks ago, and I've seen him out and about driving. Their house isn't far from mine.

"Can I call you Auntie Emmy?" Raqi asks Emersyn.

"Of course, sweetheart." My girl smiles down at her. "I need a niece to corrupt." They all laugh.

I've heard that Bas calls Ryan his uncle. I'm still not sure what their relationship is to each other. Karston said Ryan was a basket case when he and Tommy had wheeled Emersyn into the ER after her attack. He wasn't quite as bad as he was with Jas but close. According to Karston, Ryan even told the other physician on duty they had to treat her because he couldn't.

The match is about to start. Hays still hasn't been cleared to play, so he's sitting on the bench. Today's game is against the team his bully is on. The thought crosses my mind as I get a strong whiff of perfume and sneeze. Emersyn turns to look at me, and I watch her face fall as Hilary sits next to me and touches my arm.

"Where are we going to dinner tonight?" Hilary asks, and I look at her in shock.

"What?" Brooklyn says from next to me. He stands and moves to sit with Koda. Damn it, there went my buffer.

"Where are you taking me tonight?" she says loud enough for others to hear. I look at Emersyn, but she won't look at me. Ryan, however, is shooting daggers at me.

"I have no clue what you're talking about. I'm not taking you out. Never asked you and never will." My voice booms. I want Emersyn to hear, don't need her to get the wrong impression.

Emersyn turns to look back at Ryan, and Jasmin is now giving me the evil eye. Jas stands up as I hear Emersyn ask if they can move.

"No, we aren't moving because he's being a dumbass," Ryan says, and I glare at him.

"How could you?" Jasmin is standing in front of me now. "She's a sweet person, and you are being an idiot. You know Ryan is faithful to me."

"Go sit down, little girl. You already took a sexy doctor, you don't need a piece on the side." Hilary doesn't know how close to death she is as Jasmin looks at her with venom in her eyes.

"You're just jealous. You can't get any man in this town because you've either already fucked them and it was bad or because they know how fake your boobs are." Jasmin turns to move away.

"Slut," Hilary spits.

"Don't ever call her that again." Emersyn is up and in

Hilary's face. "You are a bitch who is raising a bully. You have so much Botox in your face, you can't share a true emotion. Jasmin is happily married to a sexy doctor, and you won't ever get yourself one."

I can't stand her defending Ryan.

"Sexy doctor? Are you sure you're not sleeping with him under her nose." I swing my hand toward Jasmin.

The crack of Emersyn's hand against my face is like a bucket of ice water poured over me. My words were hateful, and I didn't mean them. I reach for her to apologize.

"They are brother and sister, you asshole. I hate that everyone assumes they are more than that just because they are trying to protect me and won't tell anyone," Cynthia says, and we all turn to her.

"Mom." Emersyn moves to her and pulls her into her arms.

"Cynthia," Ryan says as he pats her back, and I turn to see Jasmin moving over to her husband. Her eyes are big, and her mouth is in a perfect O. She didn't even know the truth of their relationship.

"Oh my God." I move toward Emersyn, but she pulls away. She looks at her mother and then to Ryan.

"Tell him I got paged. I have to go." She runs from the arena, and I'm shocked.

"You just couldn't leave it alone, could you." Ryan advances on me. "I knew you were a dumbass, but this is top of the pile shit. She likes you, probably loves you, but you couldn't stop yourself."

"I couldn't stand hearing her say you were sexy." I

can't believe I confessed that. I want to go after her but can't because Lorelei isn't here to take care of the boys.

I sit there through the entire game and wait until the boys come out of the locker room. I fake everything. I smile and congratulate them on their win, but I don't say any more. I thump Bas on his back and hate when his face falls because his mom is not here. She left because of me.

I'm a jealous fool.

# Chapter Nine

TREVOR

I tried to find Emersyn. I even tried using my membership on the board to get her information. I called Jasmin, who refused to talk to me. Ryan hung up on me. I've screwed this up majorly.

It's been a couple of days, and I watch as she moves toward her car. From here I can see how tired she is. I'm not sleeping very well either. I climb out of my truck and move toward her.

"Syn." My voice chokes as I say her name. She turns and is about to jump in her car. "Please let me explain," I beg her. She stops and turns to look at me. "I'm an asshole. You called him sexy, and I saw red. For the first time ever, I got jealous of another man, because of you. Like you got jealous of Hilary asking me out, I got jealous thinking that Ryan knew the sounds you make when you come. That he's touched you. I hate the thought that Bas's father has touched you, or any of your other Doms. I want to be your one and only. I'm in love with you. I want to be with you all the time. I lie in my bed at night and think of you. I miss you."

She stands there for a moment. "You love me? How when you've hurt me?"

"I did, and like I stated, I'm an asshole. Forgive me. Let me take you to dinner tonight. I'm not on shift, it's Tuesday." I remind her of our day.

"I can't. I can't do this. What happens the next time you get upset?"

"There won't be a next time."

"How can you say that? You know I'm friends with Sawyer. I'm friends with Collin. What about the guys on your team?"

"None of them matter. It's just you and me." I move toward her, and she doesn't back up. "I've never been in love before. I didn't realize how crazy it made me that you weren't giving me the time of day. You were avoiding me. And then you showed up with Ryan and sat near me, and I was hanging on every word you said. I want you. I need you. I won't do it again. I've realized what a fool I was." I cage her in against her car. "I'm sorry your mom had to say that in front of everyone." She looks up at me and I see the pain in her eyes.

"It was the worst thing for my mom. She and my dad had separated for a bit, and she slept with Brent. She regretted it instantly but even more when she and my dad got back together. Then she found out she was pregnant with me. She told my dad the truth, and he said he didn't care. Brent had only slept with my mom to get back at my dad because they didn't like each other. She was an ICU nurse and hadn't given Brent the time of day until then. They say it only takes one time, and I'm proof of that statement. I'm her reminder every day of my life of her worst decision. But my dad wouldn't let her think that. He couldn't have kids, so this was his way. My dad's name—the man who raised me and who I consider my father—is on my birth certificate. I wouldn't have known if I hadn't done a blood test experiment in high school. There was no way I could have the blood type I do with my parents. They confessed, and I went after Ryan." She stops and presses her head into my chest. Something soothes in me having her this close and not pushing away. Plus, she's touching me.

"Ryan hadn't known either. We both went to the same private school. I slapped him and was going to beat him up after I found out." She laughs bitterly. "He didn't raise a hand to me. He looked at me and said he had always wanted a little sister." From that day forward we kept the secret, and we stayed close, even after my dad moved us to Boston. Brent was getting suspicious of me. I tell people I look like my dad, but I don't really. I can't. I look like Ryan's dad and a bit like him."

I look down at her and realize she's right. She has the olive complexion from her mom, but she has Ryan's nose.

"Ryan has more of his mother's family's coloring. I'm a true Robert's lookalike."

I lift her chin. I can't stop myself and lower my head,

giving her time to pull away, but she doesn't. I don't care about all that anymore. Now that I know I don't have to be jealous of Ryan, I just want to make things right with her.

My lips slide across hers. Once. Twice. On the third slide, she opens, and I dive in. I press her into the side of the car more and grip her thick hair. I tip her head back so I can take the kiss deeper. My tongue slides against hers and she does the same. She rocks against me, her tongue playing with mine. I pull back and look down at her swollen lips and flushed skin.

"I've wanted to kiss those sexy as fuck lips since the first moment I saw you in the club." She smiles at my comment and it takes up her whole face. "Let's go get some dinner."

"I need to call my mom and let her know."

"Okay." I help her into her car and step back. She turns the key, and nothing happens. I take a close look at her car when she looks back at me in shock. There is a pool of fluid beneath her vehicle.

"Step back, baby," I say as I lean down and take a better look. Both tires on the passenger side are flat. Fuel and I suspect brake fluid are leaking from the bottom of her car. I pull my phone from my pocket and dial 911.

I hear her on the phone telling her mom she's with me and what is going on. She makes sure Bas is okay and then hangs up.

We don't make it out to dinner, but she takes me to her condo, where I ask Bas if I can date his mom.

"Are you going to hurt her again?" He's so protective of her. "Uncle Ryan said I'm the man of the house and need to protect my mom and grandma, but he said he has a team on her too." His words give me pause and I dial Ryan.

"You have a team on Emmy?" I say in way of greeting.

"You can't call her that. Yes, I have all my family under some kind of protection."

"Not me anymore," Jasmin says in the background.

"Most especially you," he growls in response to her. "Why?" His question is directed at me.

"Emmy's car was vandalized today. Also, I apologized to her, and we are dating now, so get over it."

"Hurt her again and they won't find your body."

"I have my own sister, so I get it. I love her, and I'm not going to hurt her."

"Okay, I'll accept that for now. I'll call my company and find out what they know." He hangs up, and I turn toward Cynthia as she walks out of her room.

"I'm so sorry you had to say that on Saturday."

She walks over to me and looks me up and down. "Don't be an asshole again. It was time. Brent and Tai are both dead now. Ryan's mom has known for years. The kids can tell people, there is no one left to protect. For the longest time I didn't want to give Brent that satisfaction. I hated that he used Emmy against Ryan, as it was. She was two years younger, and Brent would ask Ryan why he couldn't specialize like she had. It was awful. Tai worked in the ER too."

"Brent sounds like an asshole."

"He was," both Cynthia and Emmy say at the same time.

"I'm going to bed, Mom." Bas walks in and kisses his mom on the cheek. As he's moving toward me to give me a hug, his cell phone in his hand vibrates and we all look at him.

"If that is either of my boys, they are grounded. It's too late to be texting," I bark.

"Bas, your phone is supposed to be in my room on the charger," Emmy says and holds out her hand.

"I know, but I wanted to tell Hays and Dyne it finally happened."

"What happened?" I ask, confused.

"You two are dating. We are going to be brothers now, just like we want to be," he says as he hands the phone to his mom. "Tell them I'm heading to bed, but I told them that when I messaged."

She looks at the phone, and I watch as the color drains from her face. I jump up from the stool at the bar and move into the kitchen, where she has been warming up food for us.

"What is it, baby?" I take the phone from her and look at the text message.

DAD

You will be coming back to me. She can't protect her sissy boy forever.

I take a screenshot of it, then I send it to myself. Emmy

asks me to send her a copy so she can send it to her attorney.

"What was it?" Bas asks, and I turn to him as I pocket the phone.

"Let me and your mom hold on to this. It's okay. Head to bed, buddy."

"If it's my dad, he's been sending me messages for a few days." He shocks us, and I pull out the phone and look. Sure enough, he has been. He is terrorizing his own kid. Asking him for money. Begging for forgiveness. I'm disgusted by it.

"I'll get you a new phone in the morning," Emmy says, and I pull her into me tighter.

I wait until they all leave. I know what she's going to say. She moves away from me and I'm on her.

"I think we should wait to start dating until they find Caleb. I don't want your boys or family to get hurt by him."

Emersyn

Trevor advances on me, pinning me to the counter.

"I fucking told you I love you. I know you haven't said it back and I get it, but, baby, I'm not letting you go. Ryan has a team on you, and I'm going to let hospital security know what's going on." He takes my face in his hands and holds it tight. "I've tasted these beautiful lips. I've tasted your sweet pussy and fucked you sideways. I'm never letting you go. I'm addicted already."

His words are dirty and turn me on, but they also soothe me. It's exactly what he would say and what I needed to hear.

"Okay."

We eat dinner, and he takes off after promising to pick me up in the morning for work. I tried to tell him my mom could drop me off, but he wouldn't listen to me.

I fall asleep for the first time in weeks dreaming of him and what he said. Don't get me wrong, I've dreamed of him, but it wasn't the same. This time I know next week we are going to the club again. He told me. I'm excited and can't wait for the long-awaited release my body needs.

# Chapter Ten

EMERSYN

Even though Trevor works nights, he has been at my condo every day since Tuesday to take me to work. Today he's off and wants to have a sleepover at his house. I'm not sure we should do this yet, but we'll see. The boys all have hockey games. I can't believe it was just last week that we were here at the arena and I thought it was completely over. All the family is here again too. Even Lorelei, who looks exhausted. She has to work tonight. She tells her brother she's working at a new place, some club but doesn't share more other than the last bar wasn't paying her enough.

Bas is on the ice, along with Dyne, and they are playing really well. I watch as Bas defends his net from an attack.

"Bitch, where is my money?" a man yells. I recognize the voice.

I look down the bleachers to see Caleb standing in front of the glass. He looks strung out. He was addicted to pain meds before, maybe never stopped. I caught him once trying to steal a prescription pad from me. Thank goodness I did before he could really ruin me.

"Watch your mouth," Trevor growls, and he and Ryan are on their feet. The play on the ice stops as everyone is paying attention to us now.

"I want my money. I put up with your fat ass and the whiny titty baby for five years. I deserve some compensation," he yells again, and I stand. I need to get him out of here before he hurts Bas more than he already has.

"I don't have to pay you anymore; it's been five years. You don't get child support anymore either. You haven't seen him in months, and I know you hurt him." I'm not scared of him anymore. He can't take my son away from me, and I have a wonderful man at my side now.

I make my way down the bleachers. When I'm almost to him, I'm lifted off my feet and turned around. Trevor gently sets me on the row behind him.

"You are not going anywhere near him, beautiful." Trevor stands between us.

Ryan storms down and faces off with Caleb. "If you were more of a man, you wouldn't need to take her money. If you were more of a man, you'd take care of yourself and not still live at home with Mommy and Daddy."

"I see you're sniffing after her too. Haven't tapped that whale yet?" Caleb swings on Ryan, who deflects the hit and pins him to the glass.

I catch a glimpse of Bas's face. He's actually got a smile on his face seeing his father taken care of. The police arrive and take Caleb into custody. Once everything settles down and I needlessly apologize for the interruption, the game resumes. I hope nothing else happens. I can't take any more.

After the game we get a phone call from the police department. They confirm it was Caleb who vandalized my car, but he won't confess to the attack. I'm sure he will with time. But right now I'm more focused on the fact that Trevor is pulling up to the house I've driven past several times. He turns up the driveway, and I take in the exterior of the home. I love the rock walls and the large windows. One part of the house is even shaped like a turret on a castle.

"Where are we?" I look at Trevor.

Lorelei pulls past us in her car and into the two-car garage facing us. Trevor turns his truck toward the three-car garage and pulls into the last bay.

"This is my house." His deep voice and chuckle cause my body to respond. We haven't done more than kiss since we made up on Tuesday, and my body is craving him.

"I've driven past this house a couple of times because I love the exterior and wanted to look inside," I confess.

The twins and Bas chuckle from the back seat, and I look back at them.

"It's true. She was going to stop one day and ask who the builder was. Grammy told her to just let it go."

"Well, I'm glad you like it. Stay put. I'll come get you and show you around."

I watch his big body move around the truck and can't

help myself as I think of what tonight could mean for us. Once he's opened my door and helped me down, he looks over my head and then pins me to the side of the truck. His lips take mine in a deep kiss before he lifts me up with a grip on my ass cheeks. I moan into his mouth when I feel his hard cock through both of our jeans.

"I fucking needed a taste, Syn. I can't wait to get you naked and in my bed tonight." His voice is deeper and vibrates through his chest against my nipples.

"I can't wait either." I sigh as he lowers me to my feet.

"Come on, before one of those boys comes looking for us."

We walk hand in hand to the door and are stepping through when a large Great Dane bounds for us. The dog is black except for a patch of white on his chest. He tries to push past Trevor but stops when Trevor issues a command.

"Bane, sit," he orders, and the dog plops down. His long legs and big body are still intimidating in this position, but it's better than him up on all fours. "This is Bane. He'll lick you to death unless you're hurting the boys or Lorelei. He'll probably become protective of you too, baby." He takes my hand and holds it out, palm down, for Bane to sniff. I'm trying not to freak out. Bas has always wanted a dog, but this guy is a beast. He sniffs my hand and then licks it. His thick tail brushes the floor, hitting the wall in his excitement.

"That way is how you get to Lorelei's place from the inside. It goes through the other garage." He points to a long hall to our left. At the open door next to us, he hollers down. "Boys, call Bane."

One of the twins calls him, and the dog takes off down the stairs. We move along the hall we are standing in, heading deeper into the house. He points out the laundry room hidden behind a door. We keep moving and he stops at a closed door.

"I'll show you that room last, it's ours."

He turns to the right, to a door before "our" room. Butterflies take flight in my stomach at him calling it that.

The room he leads me into now is amazing. It's a large great room, breakfast nook, and kitchen all in one. It has huge floor-to-ceiling windows that look out over an expansive backyard. I can even see the coast in the distance. There's a pool, sporting equipment, swing set, and so much more back there. The grill area has a sink and small bar.

I turn back to the room and take it all in. The kitchen has an island with bar stools. All the appliances are modern and stainless steel. The breakfast nook contains a midsize table and chairs. But the great room has the largest sectional sofa I've ever seen. It faces the fireplace and a large screen television above it. The exposed beams give it a rustic feel that I absolutely love. All the decorations are functional and modern looking. The sectional is a deep charcoal color, perfect for kids and pets.

"What do you think?" he asks with pride in his voice. "My parents gave me access to some money they had put back for me to get this place built. After Portia left and I realized I needed help, I knew the apartment I was in wouldn't cut it for growing boys."

I smile at him. "I get it. This place is nice. How many bedrooms?"

"With the mother-in-law apartment, it's a total of six. There are a total of six and a half baths too. Each of the boys has their own bathroom. Want to see?" He doesn't wait for me to respond but drags me through the great room to the first bedroom.

"Brooklyn's." He points to a door facing the back of the house. Brooklyn's name is on the door.

A door in front of us is open and I see the half bath he was talking about. He leads me back through the great room to the other side of it and shows me two more bedrooms. These have each of the twins' names on the doors. A small hall connects them. He turns to where I saw the round window room and steps through the door. It's a library with a large desk in it.

"This could be your office," he says with hope in his voice, and I look up at him.

"Trevor, I don't know if we are there yet." I want to be, but I'm so scared.

"I know, baby. Come on." We pass the large double door entrance to the home. "This could be a dining room." He shows me to a room on the other side of the doors. "I use it for the boys to do their homework in." Sure enough, there are three desks and maps with other posters on the walls. "We'd have to add a desk for Bas." His voice clogs with emotion. "Just think about it, baby. Lorelei has been saying she wants to move out. Your mom could move into her place."

"Give me some time." I sigh as he pulls me into his arms for a deep kiss. He then leads me back through the house to where we started and takes me downstairs.

"Guest room and gaming room," he says. I take in the pool table, foosball, television, and another large sofa, where the younger boys are currently playing games on a video game system.

"Are you ordering pizza?" Brooklyn asks from the recliner he's stretched out in while playing on his phone. He looks up when his father doesn't answer him. "Sorry, Dad. Can you order pizza?" he asks again, this time paying attention to his father and not his phone.

"Yeah, I'll get it ordered now. Anything special you want?" Trevor turns to look at me, and I can't hide my joy. He knows what Bas likes, but he's asking me personally, not assuming.

"I'll eat whatever you are getting." I lean into him.

"Ew," all four boys exclaim as I go up on my tiptoes to kiss his chin and feel his beard tickling my face.

"She likes chicken bacon ranch or Greek style," Bas tells him, and I feel Trevor's lips tip up against mine.

"Got it, little man." He leans down and throws me over his shoulder. "Brook, order it and use my credit card. We'll be back." He heads up the stairs and moves to "our" bedroom. When he kicks the door closed, I push against his back to look around.

There's a big king-size bed and a sofa in front of the

large windows that look out at the backyard. Everything is in creams and browns.

"My mom and sister decorated, but you can change anything you want."

"I like it," I tell him truthfully. He lifts me up and drops me on the bed. He is over the top of me before I can move.

"Like it? Baby, I want everything in this house to show you live here too, along with Bas. Since our first night together, I've wanted you right here." His confession takes my breath away.

I can't hide my emotion, and I lean up and kiss him on his soft, smooth lips. He takes over the kiss, burying his hands in my hair, and takes me higher and deeper. I hook my leg around his hip and grind myself against him. I'm so turned on. I don't realize his phone is ringing until he pulls back and I hear him growl into it.

"What?" He pauses and looks down at me. "Okay, we're on our way." He stands up, and I watch him adjust himself. I lie there longer, taking him all in. "Come on, babe, your condo was broken into." His words are a bucket of ice and I jump up.

After we let Lorelei know what's going on, we head out. I'm worried about my mother until I see her standing outside our home in the hall.

"Mom!" I rush to her and hug her tight to me.

"I wasn't here. I went to lunch with Ry and Jas." She looks me over and smiles. I guess my hair is still mussed from our make-out session.

Ryan is standing behind her.

"Security called me. I came and then called Trevor." I nod at him.

"It's bad," my mom says, and I can't stop the full shiver that runs down my body.

"He must have done it before he came to the arena," Ryan adds, and I turn to enter my condo. "No don't, Emmy. You don't want to see what he did."

"I do." I push past the cops, and I'm floored.

Trevor

My gut twists in fear when I see what he did to her place. It means she'll be with me sooner, and I'm happy for that, but I'm upset for her because he destroyed so much of their stuff. Each room is full of hate spray-painted on the walls and garbage. The police ask the building security for camera footage. Once they've processed the place, they allow us to gather as much of their stuff as we can. Most of Emersyn's clothes are destroyed. Her bed was slashed apart.

Her mother's room has destruction, but her clothes are at least not in pieces. Bas's room has holes in the walls and hate spewed in paint. Emersyn cried the hardest at the sight of her son's room. She said most of it was replaceable and that a good majority of their stuff was in storage, so they still have things. But seeing what he wrote on his own son's walls is disturbing. I don't know what train this guy is on, but it seems like it's the crazy train.

When we finally get home, the boys are all in the living room watching movies. Lorelei had to head to work, so Jas sent Koda over to sit with them. Brook hated it. But even though Caleb is in jail, his friend is still out there. I didn't want to risk leaving the boys alone, even if Ryan had a team sent to sit on the house for extra precaution while we dealt with the condo.

I'm not loaded like Ryan is, but I'm going to find out what security company he's using and hire them myself. The thought of Emmy, Bas, or any of my family hurt makes me crazy. I warm her up a plate of pizza, but she just picks at it. I need to get her mind off of everything. She's been concerned about where they are going to stay, but I've already got that planned. Ryan is having Cynthia stay with him for now. They won't be able to return to the condo until a cleaning company comes in and does a major cleanup.

"Come on, baby." I pull her hand toward our room. "Strip and head for the bathroom," I order her once we're inside. She knows I'm using my Dom voice because she instantly perks up. I head back out to the living room. "Bed after this movie," I tell the boys, and Koda says he'll head home afterward too.

When I return to our room, she is naked on her knees waiting for me in the bathroom. I strip and move to the large shower and kick on all the sprayers. I tilt her chin up to look at me. Her eyes meet mine and I almost get lost in the hazel color. When her eyes drop to my cock, it flexes against my belly.

"Please, Sir," she begs.

"You may."

She reaches for my cock and licks the drop of pre-cum from the tip. I lock my knees when she sucks me deep into her mouth so I don't drop. The bathroom is slowly filling with steam as she slides her mouth up and down my shaft. If I don't stop her, I'm going to come in her mouth when I want to come deep in her pussy. I want to feel her against me, skin to skin. We aren't at the club, and I can do that finally.

"Enough." The word comes out in a hoarse gasp.

She releases me and leans back on her feet again. I reach down and pick her up. I need her taste on my tongue and to get her primed before I take her. I carry her into the shower stall and set her on the bench before dropping to my knees in front of her. Her head falls back as I trace my finger through her wet heat.

"I'm going to take this pussy bare tonight, Syn. I've been dreaming of doing that for a long time. Feeling your tight, wet heat against my cock."

"I have an IUD." She confirms what I already know is in her profile.

I lean forward and spread her knees wider to accommodate my shoulders. Just before I lick her, I give her my truth. "Once I get my ring on your finger, we will be discussing that. We need a little girl for all these boys to protect."

I lick her from top to bottom, my tongue spearing into her. She cries out and grips my hair tight in her fists. I proceed to eat her as if I was starved. In fact, I've been starved for her taste, it's been so long. I've needed her. I don't let up as I fuck her with my tongue and suck on her clit until she is pulling back from me. She orgasms right away, and I let her come because I know she needed that. Tonight is about proving how much I love her and how much I want to keep her.

I move back to her clit and suckle it, running my tongue over it's hard nub as I spear two fingers into her tight pussy. When she screams, I reverse our positions. Placing her on my lap, I enter her in a long slide. Her head falls back and I kiss down her neck and suck each breast into my mouth. She takes over and rides me. My grip on her waist tightens as I try to hold off what is about to happen. I don't want it to stop. She feels better than I ever imagined. As my balls pull up, ready to explode, I bite her nipple gently and she comes again. I pump her up and down my cock a couple more times before I plant myself deep and come hard. My cum splashes across her insides, making me want to thump my chest knowing she's mine. Her head falls to my shoulder, and my head falls back against the glass. We sit like that for a bit before I help her stand and we rinse off.

When I fall asleep, she's naked in my arms and everything feels perfect. I couldn't imagine anything else coming between us.

# Chapter Eleven

EMERSYN

I don't want to say it's official, but as of last Saturday, Bas and I moved in with Trevor and the boys. It's been almost a week of bliss, but I still worry about the other shoe dropping. My mom is still at Ryan's. She's close enough though that if Lorelei is working and we need her, she can be here.

Tonight it's just me and the boys. Trevor is working and I'm having a game night with them. Tuesday Trevor and I went to the club and had some fun letting off steam. Every morning I kiss him goodbye as he walks in from work. He's actually talking about switching to a day shift but doesn't want to leave JD and Karston. I told him I'm okay with his schedule and don't mind him working nights. It gives me more time to get to know his boys.

Lorelei seems to be going through some stuff that she won't talk to me about. I hope soon she'll feel comfortable with me, like a sister. In the last week my feelings for Trevor have only deepened.

"I'll buy Park Place," Brook says as he looks at Hays, who is playing banker.

My cell phone rings, and I see the hospital number flashing across the screen.

"Dr. St. James," I answer.

"We have a pediatric case coming in ambulance. Status is it's a compound fracture of the forearm."

"I'll be there as soon as I can." I hang up the phone and look at the boys, who are all watching me. "Sorry, guys, I have to run. I'll have Grandma Cynthia come stay with you. It will be a late night." I know just from the description it's going to require surgery.

I dial my mom as I move to the bedroom to change out of my lounge pants and Trevor's T-shirt. "I got called in for an emergency," I tell her as I dress in black slacks, a white button-down, and top it with a black-and-white pullover sweater. The fall air is getting chillier the further into November we go. I slip my heels on and head out to kiss the boys good night. All four of them, including Brooklyn, like me hugging them. Trevor's boys have been starved for a mother's love, even though they have Lorelei and Trevor's mom. They like me hugging and giving them kisses on the cheek or forehead. Every time I kiss their foreheads, I remember Trevor doing that to me and I realize how much affection is in the move.

I'm about to let Trevor know I got called in when my cell goes off again.

"Dr. St. James," I answer via Bluetooth in the car.

"Emmy, you're going to want to get here. It's a previous patient, and she has other injuries." Ryan's voice comes across the line.

"Shit. Who?" I ask, worried I already know.

"Bailey," he confirms, and I start rattling off treatment suggestions as I pull into the employee parking lot minutes later.

"I'm here. I'll be in shortly." Reaching into my purse, I pull out my badge so I can hurry. I run from the car to the employee entrance, leaving my cell and purse behind in my rush.

I enter the ER and grab a lab coat from the general locker room and clip on my badge. I head straight to Trauma 1, where Ryan said they were. Karston and his new partner, Tommy, are still here giving their report. I look at Bailey and my heart breaks. Her little body is bruised and broken. I hold in the sob and get to work, helping the doctor and nurses stabilize her.

"Where is her mom?" I ask the room and notice Ryan isn't present.

"In Trauma 2 with Dr. Reynolds," a nurse responds.

We get Bailey stabilized and ready to go to imaging when a loud pop sounds through the ER. People are screaming and yelling before a man bursts into the trauma room. He fires a gun, and I curve my body over Bailey's to protect her. She has tears in her eyes and is trying to talk to me. I shake my head to stop her. The gun goes off again. I need to do something.

"Stop shooting," I say loudly. "There are too many gases in here. Do you want to blow yourself up too?"

"I'm going to kill you, just like I did my bitch wife."

I recognize his voice instantly. He's the man who attacked me in the pizza parlor parking lot. Bailey's father was probably going to use me to get to them. That's why he attacked me. It's the only explanation.

"Come here now, you fucking bitch, or I shoot the kid." He points the gun at the bed. I've still got my body between him and her, but I'm not draped over her as I was before.

"No, don't, Emmy." I hear Ryan, but I have to think of the patient.

I move toward him, and he yanks me by the arm when I'm within reach. He spins me around and puts the gun to my head, using me as a shield.

"Look, I'm right here. Let these others go. They don't deserve to be hurt for something you're mad at me for." I assume he's mad at me. He laughs, and the sound is bitter.

"Get out, or I kill her," he yells, and people are moving.

Nurses start pushing beds. A nurse grabs Bailey's bed and starts to move her. Ryan passes in front of the room we are in, pushing Bailey's mom's bed.

"Not her or her mother," Bailey's father says and fires the gun next to my ear.

I cry out and cringe. When I don't feel anything, I look and see a nurse on the ground holding her side.

"Let me treat her," I beg, but he doesn't let me go.

He smacks the gun against my head and then points it at Ryan. I can't let him shoot him. He has a family who needs him.

"No, not him. He can treat her." I hear the emotion in my voice and clear my throat. I need to sound firmer so this guy doesn't know how much Ryan means to me.

"Dr. St. James," Ryan starts, but the gun goes off again.

I scream and look at Ryan. He's uninjured, but the bullet struck Bailey's mom. Ryan moves to help her, and the guy fires the gun again.

"I said not her. Leave her and get the nurse." He points at the nurse on the floor.

Ryan moves past us and the guy backs up, pulling me away from Ryan. I watch as Ryan carefully lifts the nurse into his arms and carries her to a waiting gurney.

"Move my wife into here too," the guy orders a couple of technicians, and they do as he says. Bailey looks over at her mom and starts crying harder. I'm pretty sure her mom is not going to make it. I need to keep Bailey safe.

After some time and insisting, security finally clears the ER. They didn't like leaving me with him and two patients, but they couldn't put any more people at risk. Once the ER is clear, I try to come up with a plan. If I can keep a level head, maybe I can get the upper hand here.

"Let me check their vitals and make sure they are okay," I say once he calms behind me.

"Fine, but they are just going to die, like you and I will before this is all over."

His words hurt. I'm never going to see my family or Trevor again. I'm not going to have the happily ever after that was finally in my grasp. I could have had some good times already if I hadn't pushed Trevor away so much.

I push those thoughts out of my head and try to figure out how to save all of us.

Trevor

JD pulls the ambulance up to chaos. The main part of the hospital is on lockdown, and the ER has been evacuated. Patients are everywhere in the parking lot. Doctors and nurses are trying to help as more paramedics show up on scene to help stabilize or transport patients to the next town over. The helicopter is on standby if needed.

Rumors are a gunman has taken over the ER. They say a doc and two patients are still in there with him. I'm glad my girl is home safe with the boys.

"Trevor." I hear my name as I step out of the ambulance. Both Karston and Ryan are walking toward me and my gut clenches.

"It's Emmy," Ryan says, and I drop. My knees slam into the pavement and my head falls. I scream into my fists and then come up fighting. I need to get to my girl. Police tackle me to the ground and Karston is on top of me. When my vision clears, I see Ryan looking at me with a black eye and concern on his face.

"Why? Why is she here?"

"It's a pediatric patient and her mother. A previous patient of Emersyn's," Ryan says. "The gunman is the father and spouse. He wanted Emmy from the get-go. He said he came there for her."

"We brought in the mom and her seven-year-old. The mom was beaten within an inch of her life. The kid had a broken arm and was beaten too. They told us the perp was not on scene, so we transported," Karston tells me. I notice police and security are on hand too.

"Ryan." I hear a woman's voice and turn to see a tall, slender woman walking toward us. She moves smoothly in heavy boots. She's flanked by two large men.

"Ridley," he says.

"The guys couldn't get in there to help, but we can try to sneak them in before the cops act," she says. I'm not sure if she's being serious or not.

"Trevor, this is my friend Ridley." Ryan introduces us. "She's in charge of the security team that's been on Emmy."

Ridley reaches out to shake my hand and I just stare at it. "Why didn't they stop this?" She pulls her hand back at my words and shakes her head.

"We can't operate on the hospital premises. He was already in the ER before they could get in there. But I'm willing to break the rules and go in if you say you want me to." She pops her chin at me.

I look at the police, who are now trying to establish

contact. If this attacker came for Emersyn, there is only one outcome here. He's going to kill them all.

"That's a dumbass question. Fuck yes, I want you to get her back." I clench my jaw.

"Give me a moment to work up a good plan and we'll go in." Ridley moves away with her team to plot. The guys and I move toward them and listen in.

"We know that ER as good as the staff does. What can we do?" Karston offers. "I'm former military." JD and I look at him in shock. That last bit of information isn't something Karston shares very often.

An hour later we have a plan and Ridley is ready to go in. I pray this works and they can rescue my girl.

# Chapter Twelve

EMERSYN

I've got Bailey stabilized and pain meds running through her IV. He was going to deny me doing that, but I told him it was better for all of us if I did. That she would start crying more if I didn't. I move to Bailey's mom and start assessing her.

"Dr. St. James," she says softly. I lean down to listen to her.

"What are you doing?" He points the gun at us.

"Checking her respirations, unless you let me grab my stethoscope." I point to it on the counter where I left it.

"Get it. Shut her up."

I move toward the nurses' station where I'd left my stethoscope at some point. I see the meds already drawn up to give Bailey's mom. As I pick up the stethoscope, I pocket the needles. He's not watching me. His focus is on his wife's shallow breathing.

"Why do you want to kill us all?"

"She is worthless. The kid only cries. And you, you had to interfere." His voice is laced with pain.

I look at him and see he's bleeding too. I didn't notice it before, but now I see the blood pooling at his feet.

"Can I check you over when I get done with her?" I wave my hand toward his side.

"Doesn't matter, soon enough we'll all be dead."

I move back toward his wife. He doesn't interrupt me when I lean over her this time.

"Promise me you'll take care of my Bailey," she says softly.

"We're going to get out of here, and you will take care of her yourself," I respond, my lips barely moving so he doesn't know.

"We both know that's a lie. I'm dying. Please take care of my baby."

I nod. She's right. We're losing her. Her lung is filling up with blood.

"I need to help her. She needs surgery."

He moves over toward us, and I step back, not wanting him to get a hold of me again. I reach into the pocket with the meds and pull off the caps, exposing the needles. They are only pain meds, but if I can impair him enough to get us out of here, it's better than waiting for him to put a bullet in my head.

"You ready to die, you sorry ass bitch." He leans over her, and I pull the syringes free and stab them into his leg. I push the plungers down as he rears back. He smacks me hard enough I fall to the floor. He raises the gun, and I close my eyes.

"I love you, Trevor." I say the last thing I want on my lips as the gunshot rings out.

I don't feel pain or burning. I open my eyelids and look straight into his lifeless eyes. A woman strides into the room and reaches down for me.

"Come on, Trevor is waiting." She helps me up, and I stand there for a moment.

"What about them?" I turn to look at Bailey and her mom. The woman moves to Bailey's mom, and I go to Bailey. "The mom needs surgery."

"Yeah, but you can't do it right now." When she doesn't say more, I look at her and she shakes her head. "You wait here, I'll let them know it's safe." She moves out of the room toward the back of the ER. I wait, and when nurses and other doctors start rushing in, I give them my report.

"I'll be back, Bailey," I tell her as she looks at me with tears in her eyes. I want to hold her, but until we get those images, she has to stay immobile in the cervical collar.

I head for the exit and see Trevor walking straight for me. Ryan is walking in behind him, letting Trevor come to me first.

I rush toward him and jump at him.

"I love you. I want to move in. I want babies with you," I cry into his neck as he holds me tightly to his chest.

Trevor

Her words only settled me a little bit. I haven't left her side since she jumped into my arms, not even when she went back in to stabilize Bailey for surgery in the morning. Child services is strongly taking her mother's deathbed request into consideration. I'm confident we will be getting her. I look over at my woman sitting in the passenger seat of her car. We are heading home, where the boys saw the news and know what happened. I need to hold her and make sure she's really alive. I can't believe how close it came. When she told me, I wanted to take a gun from the many cops and shoot him again. He died instantly. Ridley put a bullet right between his eyes.

When Emersyn was questioned, she could only say that a team of soldiers saved her. She didn't mention it was a woman, and because she didn't have a name, she couldn't tell them more than that.

"What was her name?" Her voice is scratchy from exhaustion and talking so much.

"Ridley. Your brother knows her."

"I want to thank her." She hiccups and then starts to cry. She hasn't shed a tear until now, not even as she was telling me how much she loves me. I pull her car into the garage and then walk around to lift her out. All the boys are waiting for us along with Lorelei.

"Are you okay?" Bas is the first to ask her, followed by the others.

She gives them a weak, watery smile.

"I'll make some tea," Lorelei says, and moves off. I carry Emersyn into our room and right into the bathroom.

"Give us a sec," I tell the boys. I close the door and help her change into a T-shirt of mine and a pair of shorts. The shirt fits like a dress on her.

I carry her back out and sit her on the bed. The boys all climb in around her and hold her tight.

"Please don't leave us," Hays says, and I have to turn my back to the scene so they don't see the tears in my eyes.

"I'm never leaving you. I want to marry your dad and stay with you. Is that okay?"

I haven't officially asked her, just said I wanted my ring on her, but I'll take it. Whatever I can get and as fast as I can.

Cynthia joins us in the room and checks in on her daughter.

"Yes. Please, Dad, marry her," Dyne says, and Brooklyn laughs along with Bas.

"I plan to," I say as I swing back around to take them all in.

I fall asleep with her in my arms after she kisses each of the boys and her mom, assuring them all she's safe and not hurt. We don't tell them about Bailey yet because we want to make sure everyone is okay with our relationship change.

I hold her tight to my body. She wakes up crying from fear, and I soothe her and calm her. She plans to go into work tomorrow and assist with Bailey's surgery. She won't perform it because of her nerves and because of us adopting her. Bailey is practically family.

The next morning we take all the boys and Cynthia to meet Bailey. I feel Emersyn cringe next to me as we move through the main entrance. She looks over to where the ER connects to the main hospital. I'm worried she's going to be afraid of being here, but I know we can all overcome this together. If we have to, we'll get her into counseling.

We get on the elevator and head up to the peds floor. At the security check-in, Emersyn shows her badge and the rest of us get placed on the list to visit Bailey. I've never been up on this floor, and I see why my wife likes being here. Yeah, I'm not wasting any time. We'll make it official soon enough. We turn down the main hall and head for the room where an officer is standing outside the door. When we step into the room, the social worker stands up.

"She had a rough night and called out for you many times."

"I'm staying with her tonight, no matter what," Emersyn says without pause. I look down at her and nod. We'll stay here with our girl.

Bailey reaches for Emmy and they embrace. The little girl is so tiny, even for seven. I told her I wanted a girl, but I still plan to knock up my Syn.

# Epilogue 1

## TREVOR

6 MONTHS LATER

"I now pronounce you husband and wife," the judge says, and I lean down to kiss my beautiful bride's full lips. She made me wait to marry her. Today is a day to celebrate. Not only is Emersyn my wife, but Bailey is officially our daughter. The judge signs the adoption paperwork next.

Bailey has come out of her shell and it's all because of her big brothers. They dote on and protect her. She hasn't been to the hospital in a long time. We've made sure she's well taken care of. My wife spoils all our kids. I've even adopted Bas today. Caleb signed off his parental rights. He pleaded guilty as part of the deal. He'll serve five years. Bas wasn't upset when I told him I wanted him. He, Bailey, and Emmy are all in counseling for everything they went through.

My sister promptly moved out a month after the situation at the hospital and moved away from Eastport. I'd found out she was bartending at the Satin Room. I couldn't tell her no because she's an adult, but something happened and she up and quit there and left. Erika and Leif won't tell us what happened. They say it had something to do with another member. We all miss her, but she's been upset for a while, and I don't know how to fix it. The last postcard we got from her was from Paris. She's using her trust fund to travel.

Both Emmy and I still work, but I'm on days with JD now. Turns out he wanted to switch up schedules as well. Emersyn shared that she has money too, and together we don't have to work, but we like to. So we are staying employed. I'm worried we are going to have to get a bigger house or add on more rooms if we do have a baby.

Ryan and Jas are taking all of the kids to their place tonight. Raqi and Bailey have become really close friends. Plus, they owe us. We've babysat overnight for them, including little Grant.

A couple hours later I'm driving my wife from her brother's place to ours. I look over at her and see a huge, content smile on her face.

"What are you smiling at, Mrs. Myer?" I ask her as I turn my attention back to the road.

She sighs. "I was thinking of how much fun we had at our combo bachelor-bachelorette party last month." I wouldn't let her and the girls go out, and neither did the other girls' men. So we had a combination party and all of us ended up at the club later.

"That was a lot of fun. But we need to be careful. If we keep breaking the rules, I'll be thrown off the board." I chuckle. I took her bare at the club against the rules, even though we are married.

"Yeah, but it was a lot of fun. I like you taking me bare. I could get pregnant."

My foot comes off the accelerator and I look over at her as I pull into the driveway.

I shake my head, sure I heard her wrong as I click the button for the garage door. I pull into the middle bay and look over at my truck. I had to upgrade to a full-size SUV, seeing as we have so many kids. Even Emmy traded hers in for a full-size GMC Denali with three rows of seats. I come around to help her out, loving the beautiful pale green dress she's wearing. It brings out more of the green in her hazel eyes. I lift her up and carry her toward our room.

"Did you hear me?" She tips my face to look at her.

"I want to get you pregnant, but you said we had to wait."

"I had my IUD removed two months ago, Daddy," she says, and I almost stumble and drop her.

I push her into the wall as soon as we're in our room.

"Are you saying?"

"Yep. Must have been last month." She smiles at me, and my lips are on hers. She's everything I've ever wanted. The perfect little Syn, and she's all mine.

# *Epilogue 2*

## EMERSYN

10 YEARS LATER

I look down at the ice and see my oldest son. Brooklyn was a first-round draft pick for the Eastport Pirates Hockey team two years ago. He's the assistant captain of the team and is making a name for himself. Last season they won the cup.

Bas and Dyne are both anticipated to be high up draft picks next year. Hays doesn't want to go professional; he's talking about going to medical school and following in my footsteps.

Our family continued to grow after our daughter Alisyn was born. A couple of years later we welcomed another little girl, Lyric, who is five now. I told Trevor that was enough kids. With Bailey, we have seven. Bailey will be graduating high school in May, and we couldn't be prouder. She's already been accepted to Eastport University.

I look at my husband in our family box and smile. He is the head of the ambulance service now. He works hard to make sure each of our kids know how special and loved they are. Every night before I close my eyes, he wraps me in his arms and kisses the top of my head, then he tells me how happy he was that he found a good Syn.

"Happy, Emmy." His voice breaks me from my thoughts, and I look up at him.

"I'm very happy, husband." I smile at him as Lyric climbs into my lap.

I look around at all my family. Ryan and I changed everything when we decided to come to Rhode Island and work at Eastport General. We stepped out of the shadow of his father and away from the social statuses of Chicago. I wouldn't change anything that I've gone through to be here with my husband and kids. And this big, huge family that we all created together with a club called Satin Room.

DOCTORS of Eastport General

# About the Doctors of Eastport General

I hope you enjoyed my book, Doctor Sinful, which is part of the shared world Doctors of Eastport General.

Would you like to read all of them? Find them here on Kindle Unlimited.

Come on in and meet the new ER Physicians, Surgeons, Specialists, Residents, and patients that occupy the rooms and halls of the largest hospital on the coast of Rhode Island. You may even run into some of the doctors from Season 1. We hope you are ready to fall in love with all the new sexy stories that take place inside the walls of Eastport General Hospital.

Doctor Irresistible – Syd Ryan
Doctor Mistake – Amy Stephens
Doctor Divine – Tracy Broemmer

Doctor, Please – Celeste Granger
Doctor Frank Enstein – CA King
Doctor Change of Heart – Amber Ghe
Doctor Rescue – Mel Walker
Doctor Delectable – TL Mayhew
Doctor Love – Adryan Hart
Doctor Danger – Pandora Snow
Doctor Stuck-Up – A.N. Waugh
Doctor Sinful – E.M. Shue
Doctor Right – S.L. Sterling

**Titles from Season 1**

Doctor Heartbreak by D.M. Davis
Doctor Feelgood by Amy Stephens
Doctor D's Orderly Affair by CA King
Doctor Trouble by E.M. Shue
Doctor Temptation by Syd Ryan
Dueling Doctors by DC Renee
Doctor Sexy by TL Mayhew
Doctor Fix-It by Mel Walker
Doctor One of a Kind by Anjelica Grace
Doctor Casanova by Emma Nichole
Dirty Doctor by Amanda Richardson
Doctor All Nighter by Adora Crooks
Doctor Desire by S.L. Sterling

# Acknowledgments

To the very awesome and one of my closest writing friends, S.L. Sterling, thank you for doing another Doctors of Eastport General. Thank you for coming up with this amazing collaboration. I love my Doctor books. I love that it gave me a chance to start my new series Tattoos & Sin. All that couldn't have been done without you. Always remember I'm here if you need anything. I can't wait to work with you more in the future.

My hubby is always there supporting me and pushing me to do more. To be bigger. To stop giving away the bank. To take chances. I love you babe; you are MY pain in the butt.

My girls all three of them are there with me during planning, plotting, cover design, and even beta reading for me. Thank you all. Paige, stop working so much. I love you, Babygirl. Kelsey, you're an amazing mother, my granddaughter is well loved and growing wonderfully. Love you my Turdbutt! Dani, I'm excited to see where you turn next. I'm proud of you always. Love you Buggyboo!!

My granddaughters both are some of the reasons I write strong women. I want them to grow up and know that they don't need a man to protect them, they can do it themselves. Jayjay and Sassyfrass Neena loves you both so much.

To the men I call sons, thank you for your help with torture, guns, knives, motorcycles, and everything else you help me with. This one didn't need as much of those, but you still helped where I needed you. Thank you and love you all!

To my family (mother, brothers, fosters, nieces, nephews, cousins, aunts, uncles, those that aren't but should be, those that I call by other names and finally those I count as) all of them everywhere thank you for your kind words, support, and not blocking me. Haha

To my bestie for putting up with my calls, texts, messages, and all the crap you deal with from me. You're the best I can't wait to get another hug from you in San Diego. Maybe I should become Canadian! Haha

As always, my assume editor, this year you set a goal for me and so far, I think we are doing pretty darn good. Thank you for all you do!

Rally Pack and A-Team, you all are awesome, and I really appreciate all you do for me. Thank you for posting and ARC reading. Someday we'll meet in the real and I'll hug you if I haven't already.

To all my author and PA friends who help me with promo and questions thank you for all your support. I'm here if you ever need it.

To you the reader thank you for taking the time to read Doctor Sinful, I hope she met your expectations. Don't forget to check out my other books for more bada$$ tough girls. If you're not a Baddie come sign up for my Facebook group. https://bit.ly/EMBaddies or my newsletter Surprises https://bit.ly/SurprisesfromEM.

Finally, to that being out there some call him by name, and some don't. I call him my guide and my light. Thank you for this talent and this opportunity.

# Also by E.M. Shue

**Securities International Series**

Sniper's Kiss: Book 1

Angel's Kiss: Book 2

Tougher Embrace: Book 2.5

Love's First Kiss: Book 3

Secret's Kiss: Book 4

Second Chance's Kiss: Book 5

Sniper's Kiss Goodnight: Book 5.5

Identity's Kiss: Book 6

Hope's Kiss: Book 7

Forever's Embrace: Book 7.5

Justice's Kiss: Book 8

Duchess's Kiss: Book 9

Kiss of Submission: Book 9.5

Truth's Kiss: Book 10 (Coming August 2023)

**Knights of Purgatory Syndicate**

A Seductive Beauty

A Tortured Temptress

**Santa Claus, Indiana Stories**

Coal for Kiera: Christmas of Love Collaboration

Hanna's Valentine: A Santa Claus, Indiana Story

Hailey's Rodeo: A Santa Claus, Indiana Story

Love in a Small Town

**Caine & Graco Saga**

Accidentally Noah

Zeke's Choice

Lost in Linc

Completely Marco

Jackson Revealed

Trusting Jericho

**Mafia Made**

Her Empire: Mafia Made 2

His Rebel: Mafia Made 5

Her Exile: Mafia Made 8 (Coming September 2023)

**Tattoos & Sin Series**

Doctor Trouble

Vegas Jackpot

Doctor Sinful

**Stand-alones**

Confined Space: KB Everyday Heroes World

Until Tucker: Happily Ever Alpha World

Rocco's Atonement

Distracting David

Taliah's Warrant Officer

Forever Finn's Kisses

Discovering Tyler

Vows & Vendettas (Coming July 2023)

**Devil's Handmaidens - Alaska**

Wrecked (Coming May 2023)

**Ramsey University Series**

Virtuous

# About E.M.

E.M. Shue is an Alaskan award-winning romance author. She is proudly featured in K Bromberg's Everyday Heroes World, Aurora Rose Reynolds' Happily Ever Alpha World, KL Donn's Mafia Made Series, Susan Stoker's Special Forces Operation Alpha World, and the soon to be released Devil's Handmaidens MC Collection.

She published her first book in 2017 after having a dream that later became the Beverley Award winning, Sniper's Kiss. Since then, she has gone on to win this award three more times with different books and has published over thirty titles.

Join Surprises from E.M. to be kept up to date on all her new releases and appearances.

https://bit.ly/SurprisesfromEM

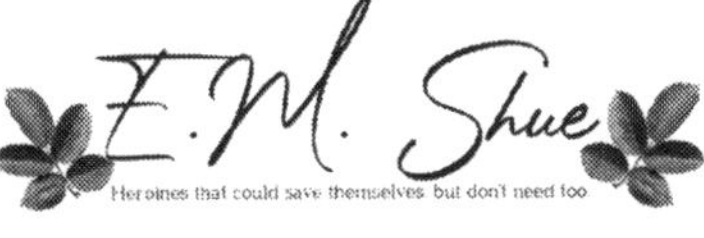

Made in the USA
Columbia, SC
18 June 2023

17636062R00085